RECON ELITE

VIKTOR ZARKOV

SEVERED PRESS

HOBART TASMANIA

RECON ELITE

Copyright © 2018 Severed Press

WWW.SEVEREDPRESS.COM

ISBN: 978-1-925711-91-2

1.

CAV V-117 landed on planet Mawholla, setting ablaze what looked like a North American pine tree. But Sam Boggs knew better, this was a long, long way from home. The SA-1 intelligence computer on Colonial Assessment Vehicle V-117 had determined Mawholla to be a forest planet, with considerable volcanic activity and cave labyrinths, but also Earth-like elevation changes (rivers and moisture in the canyons, snow and colder as you go up the mountains).

Boggs emerged from his bunk, and slipped off the virtual device connected to his Happy Box. The "Happy Boxes" made advanced space travel tolerable, as Recon Elite disappeared into their fantasies. Most of his squad chose rock star fantasies, selling out large venues while having hundreds of adoring women throw themselves at them.

Boggs chose fishing trips. Specifically the Rocky Mountains, where he'd fish streams not all that different from the ones on Mawholla. Except in the Happy Box, his wife Sarah was still at his side, before she'd died during childbirth, taking his supposed-to-be son Connor with her.

Boggs pressed the red awake button on the Happy Box chain, and soon the rest of Recon Elite Six awoke.

"Get your fat asses up," Boggs said as he slid into his forest camo uniform. "We have a planet to explore."

James T Bone rose from his bunker, rubbing his head, and his short crop of hair. He stood at 6'7, an enormous man, with the body of a WWF wrestler. Behind him, along the row of Happy Box beds rose the other four men: Jim Dagger, Raul Portman, Tim Emoth, and Mark "Pearl" Staunch.

The men rubbed their eyes, yawned, and stretched as the CAV-117 winded down its engines and began the transition into support mode.

A bay door opened, and a rush of oxygen flooded the stale cabin air.

While the fresh air flooded the cabin, a security sensor deployed numerous lasers across the opening. Sure, Recon Elite Six had been briefed, and knew much of what they were dealing with on a surface level. But Boggs again knew better, and so did the commanding officers at Colonial Preparation Base, or CPB. No matter how well recon satellites portrayed a planet, there were always surprises. A man or woman had to get onto the surface and sniff around, get his or her fingernails dirty to truly find out what the planet was all about.

There had been countless reports of snafus and surprises...many the deadly kind. And the recon satellites could not, and would never determine every species on the planet, whether said species was poisonous or hostile. Even the drones had a tough time navigating thick forest, with ancient canopies blocking out however many suns on Planet Whatever. Submersibles were launched too, plying the oceans of Mawholla.

Some of the submersibles had disappeared into underwater caves rather quickly.

A little too quickly for Boggs, as if the recon submersibles had been swallowed by something enormous.

The rest of Bogg's squad dressed, and slipped into their CR-07 replenishing backpacks. These neat backpacks regenerated a hydrating fluid of water, sodium, and carbohydrates, keeping the men consistently nourished in even the most demanding conditions for up to a week straight. The packs connected to a long over-the-shoulder straw from the top of the packs to their mouths. After that, they'd rely on on-board provisions, and whatever they could hunt and drink on Mawholla. The water had already been tested, and was approved by CPB as safe for consumption. The animals?

Not so much.

But Boggs had learned on plenty of these missions that meat was meat. If it looked like a lizard, and ran like a lizard, it probably tasted like one too, depending on what kind of vegetation the damn thing ate that week. If it had lingered in a swamp, he and his men could expect a muddy taste. If the animal had fed on meadow grasses, light and juicy. If it had fed on lichen, somewhere in-between.

"Fuck these packs," Dagger said as he stood next to Boggs. "Let's get some meat. I aint no damn vegan."

"You pussy," Emoth said to Dagger as he loaded his ZR-15, the standard colonization assault rifle for Recon Elite Six. "How in the hell did you get this job anyway? Maybe you should be a farmer."

"Hah," Portman said, also loading his ZR-15 with stun, frag, and decimate bullets. "I'd kill myself," he said as he pumped in the ammo. "I need the action."

Dagger shook his head. "Yeah, 'cause you aint had any in years."

Portman grinned and shrugged. "It's true, it's true. I lost your mother's phone number."

Dagger shot Portman a look, then grinned like a maniac. "Well, I hope she was good."

Boggs sighed. "Alright you nimrods," he said. "Recon Elite is better than high school locker talk. Respect yourselves, and in return earn respect."

"Yes sir," Dagger said, standing at attention and saluting Boggs. The rest of the men fell in line as Boggs paced the room, a waterproof map clenched in his hands.

"You see that door right there, men?" Boggs said as he leaned into his squad. "You see those protective lasers? Why do you think those exist?"

"To protect us, sir," Dagger said.

Boggs stepped over to Staunch, and made firm eye contact an inch from his face. "What about you, Staunch? Why are there a hundred interlaced lasers protecting our six right now? Do you think it's because there are rabbits and possum out there?"

"No sir," Staunch said, his hands shaking at his side.

Hmmm...Boggs thought. He didn't care for that. And Staunch had been quiet pre-trip as well, as if he'd been shaken by personal issues. Boggs didn't need that. He couldn't count how many times formerly confident and centered men had inadvertently screwed with group dynamics on missions. These kinds of psychological issues had a way of creeping up.

"You good Staunch?" Boggs asked. "Recon Elite don't get nervous."

"I'm sorry sir," Staunch said as he glanced back at the laser-interlaced bay ramp.

Boggs watched as Staunch gulped his own saliva.

"A confident squad is the best squad," Boggs said as he met eyes with the rest of his men, one by one. Boggs turned and pointed to the bay opening. The smell of pine trees wafted into the craft. "Out there, you're going to encounter who-the-hell-knows-what. Sure, some of those animals may look like ones we're familiar with. But don't be fooled. They might be poisonous. Might bite. Might spit shit at you that melts your face off. Or, they could all hold hands and sing skippety-dee-doodah. You just never know. So no slacking, got it? Your partner has your back, and you have his. We go out two by two, due to the forested nature of planet Mawholla. Listen to that word, men. Mawholla. Twice the size of Earth. Two suns, Little Blaze and Big Blaze, offset by 90 degrees. According to CPB Commanders, this is *numero freaking uno* on the list. Let's not let them down. Look sharp, be sharp, or have sharp things sink into you. Got it?"

"Yes sir!" the men shouted back in unison.

Bogs cupped his ear. "What's that, I didn't quite hear you."

"Yes sir!"

"Good," Boggs said. "That's what I like to hear."

2.

Recon Elite Six stepped off the CAV-117 and into a breezy meadow. What looked to be North American pine trees swayed in the wind. To Boggs, it felt an awful lot like Montana.

"I don't get it," Dagger said as he adjusted his LifeForm Scanner that hung off his belt. "Where the hell are the birds?"

Boggs turned and shot Dagger a look. "Who the hell says there are birds?" he said.

Dagger glanced away. "The recon craft data indicated there might be."

Boggs nodded once, and spat. "Key word there is MIGHT. The drone's sensors weren't optimal due to bad weather. But CPB was hot to get here, so here we are. Let's not let our people back on Earth down."

"Roger that," Portman said, flexing his bicep as he gripped his ZR-15.

Boggs flashed his LifeForm scanner in front of him. He didn't want his men to know that he too, had suspicions as to why there were no flying life forms such as birds. This meadow was excellent habitat. Beyond the ancient-looking pine trees, rugged mountains laced with random snowfields rose higher and higher. Boggs took a breath of the clean cool air. Not like Earth air. At all. Things had gotten too hot on the home planet. They'd fucked it up really good: oceans of plastic, the shoulder seasons disappearing, with months of long drought that killed crops and triggered widespread famine. No one was able to control it. The planet had been set on a course that was unrepairable for generations.

Boggs led the way across the meadow as moist grass dragged along his camo pants, slicking his boots. Strange insects that looked like ticks and gnats scurried along the blades of grass.

"We've got life," Boggs said. "Of the insect variety."

As expected, the hand-held LifeForm meter beeped, and gave an "all clear" indicator in the shape of a green circle. Even on other planets, green meant go.

As Boggs hiked across the meadow, clouds swirled above, clean and clear and pregnant with rain. The air here was so much different than Earth, despite similar oxygen concentrations. The difference was the absolute absence of pollution. In the modern era, this was just not something human lungs were used to. Boggs noticed he felt lighter and faster, despite a valley elevation of 3,231 feet, approximately 2,000 feet higher than his apartment in Billings back on Earth.

Mawholla's power was having its way with him, Boggs thought. He'd been on these missions before, on planets that were quite frankly, a joke compared to Mawholla: desert planets not fit for a god damn scorpion, or planets teetering between dying out completely, and still harboring a few random life forms. There were of course the sad lot of planets near Earth, solid ice, desert, and gaseous. Useless planets, really, at this stage in their existence. And Boggs had learned in all his years from space travel that planets were a lot like people. They just existed, did their own thing, and died.

In the end, that's all this was. And he and Recon Elite Six were the spearhead for humanity, necessary agents for the ultimate survival before Earth fried like an ant under a magnifying glass. Not only could Boggs feel the power of Mawholla, but he could feel the power of his men, too. Fit as bull elk thanks to years of weight training and cardio work. Boggs didn't want to say they were the "best of the best", because that was a bullshit cliché. But they were good. Real fucking good.

Boggs' LifeForm device beeped, this time revealing a yellow icon. *Caution.*

The device wasn't entirely sure what species lay before them at forest's edge.

Which sucked.

A red icon meant the animal was dangerous, take no risks. There was a sense of comfort in knowledge. But the unknown? Not so much.

The great thing about T-Bone was he loved trouble. He glanced at Boggs, and Boggs gave a thumbs up. T-Bone inched ahead to tree line, his ZR-15 aimed and ready.

The rest of the squad aimed their ZR-15s without hesitation, as if purely on instinct. Boggs raised his weapon, expecting whatever was behind the ferns to launch right at them.

But it did not.

Instead a large moose-like animal emerged slowly, its ears pinned back. But this was not quite a moose, with much smaller ears, and very narrow eyes.

And it wasn't quite healthy.

A chunk had been taken out of its rear, and the animal paced and whimpered.

"Holy shit," Emoth said, inching closer to T-Bone, who was already crouching in the grass and way too close. "Something took a hell of a bite out of this bad boy."

Blood trickled from the animal's rear flank, and glistened in the dim sunlight.

"Anyone hungry?" Portman asked as he raised his rifle.

Boggs stepped over to Portman and lowered the rifle barrel with the palm of his hand. "We don't have time for this shit," Boggs said. "We have weeks of medically-approved sustenance, and a planet to explore. We can't play gourmet chef right now."

"Gourmet?" the young Staunch asked.

"Never mind," Boggs said.

The moose-like animal limped off into deeper forest, and they never saw it again.

3.

As they hiked deeper into the wilderness, Boggs was impressed. Towering forests created an almost impenetrable canopy, as strands of moss and lichen clung to fallen logs the size of school buses. Double slats of sun punched through the canopy randomly, illuminating numerous forest insects. And in that spectacular ray over the fallen log, Recon Elite Six saw their first bird. It soared through sun rays, then into darkness, then into sun rays, so they only ever got a brief glimpse of the plumage color and other characteristics.

"Looks like a bald eagle," Dagger whispered.

"Not really," Emoth shot back. "More like a hawk."

Boggs spat, and wiped his mouth with the back of his hand. "Looks like a hybrid," he said, noticing the shorter wings, and longer tail feathers designed for maneuverability under the canopy.

"This one's an understory hunter," Boggs said.

An animal chittered from a branch, with big eyes and a furry tail.

"Squirrel," T-Bone said.

The hawk-like bird angled towards the branch. The squirrel turned to flee, but the hawk opened its beak, and spat a long, glowing strand of liquid that splattered the squirrel's fur. The squirrel let out an awful chirp and tried to flee, but the substance kept it tight to the branch. A moment later, yellow talons sunk into the squirrel's flesh, and it let out one last scream before going limp.

"Holy shit," Dagger said. "A spitting bird."

Boggs put his LifeForm device to his face, and spoke into it: "Hawk type species, talons, built for understory. Capable of spitting a sticky substance long distances. Potentially poisonous."

Boggs set the LifeForm device down and opened his backpack. From a scratch-proof silver bag, he produced lightweight foldable wrap-around goggles, and handed them out to his men.

"I feel better already," Dagger said. "Don't need that shit in my eyes."

"Tell me something I don't know," Staunch said as he watched the hawk tear apart the squirrel.

"We have a species capable of spitting a hell of a lot," Boggs said. "Meaning there might, and could be others, with varying capacities."

Staunch frowned. "I really hope this isn't a spitting planet," he said.

Boggs led his men deeper into the forest. The LifeForm meters beeped often, but indicated the animals were not dangerous, and very small.

Boggs wondered about that.

The LifeForm devices had been proven inaccurate on past missions. Headquarters was supposed to have updated them with firmware. The worst example of malfunction was the device indicating a common deer was a grizzly bear, and a gila-like animal on planet Korna (a miserable desert planet), as a standard field mouse.

You couldn't always trust technology. Sometimes you just had to go with your gut. It was 50/50 for Boggs. He trusted mankind's ability to build competent, reliable spacecraft. What he didn't trust was the technology you couldn't see, like chemicals.

But despite the LifeForm's not-so-perfect reliability rate, it was better than nothing.

Something cut Boggs off from his thoughts, and he spun to his left. At first it was like a reptilian blur. And then the thing came into focus, but not before it spat a foul white substance that traveled like a MLB pitcher's baseball, before caving in the right side of T-Bone's face.

"Fuck!" he screamed, as what was left of the wrap-around goggles melted and sizzled into the side of his face.

Staunch grabbed T-Bone by the shoulder and shoved him hard to the ground, while the rest of the squad opened fire. The creature was moved quickly, shooting from side to side, hiding behind a bus-sized fallen log, appearing, and then disappearing into the woods.

"Get ready to shoot to kill," Boggs shouted. "And hold your god damn fire until the thing shows itself again. Don't waste bullets, there's no munitions base here yet."

The men reloaded their ZR-15s. Portman used a branch to steady his aim at 12'oclcok, as Emoth pivoted and got their six.

As the smell of smoke cleared away, Boggs realized T-Bone was dead. Whatever the thing had spit was still eating his brain away. Boggs took his LifeForm device and recorded video. He wanted to sit by T-Bone's side, mourn him, give him a proper burial and all the right things. But this wasn't a right moment. If there were more of those creatures, they'd be dead soon, and they needed all the information they could get.

Knowledge was as powerful as a bullet.

Boggs kept the device steady as he scanned what was left of T-Bone's head. It was bizarre how the spit substance almost seemed to be freezing T-Bone's face, and burning it at the same time, especially at the edges, like dry ice.

When he was done, Boggs joined Portman, Dagger, and Staunch as they kept their rifles trained on the general area of the enormous fallen log. Branches cracked, and a faint hissing sound emitted. Boggs listened closer, holding his breath in the process.

There, to the north. More branches and vegetation swishing, and then to the east.

An uneasy knot of anxiety rose up Boggs' throat.

"Fall back to the CAV," he said. "NOW."

The group turned and ran back from where they'd come, with Boggs using the LifeForm device to make sure they weren't being surrounded. After an hour the metal CAV-117 glowed in the evening dusk. The sound of cracking branches and deadfall dissipated behind them as the men hurried up the ramp into the bay. Boggs flipped a red handle on the wall, and the interlaced lasers connected once more.

"Hey," Boggs said to his men. "We did what we could for him."

Boggs turned to Staunch, but something came up the ramp behind them.

"Fuck," Staunch shouted, as he raised his weapon.

The thing stopped short of the interlaced lasers, and hissed, eyeing the men as if they were cheesecake. Boggs had never seen anything like it, one part velociraptor, one part snake. The top half of the creature resembled the velociraptor, while the back end changed to a thick, python-like tail. It stood on two legs, occasionally going to all fours, and whipping its python tail against the metal frame of the CAV. Boggs walked up to it and made direct eye contact, separated only by the humming, interlaced lasers.

"What the fuck you doing, boss?" Emoth said.

The beast arched its head back and unleashed the sticky venom that had killed T-Bone, but Boggs lifted a Safety Shield, and blocked what would have been a deadly blow. Most of the poison sizzled and shot back at the creature as it caught up in the lasers.

For a moment the creature looked puzzled.

"Take him down," Boggs said. The men opened fire, pounding the creature over and over. To Boggs' surprise it managed to stay on its feet way too long. Finally, it collapsed at the base of the ramp, and took one last breath, its tongue hanging from its mouth.

"God damn," Portman said, the barrel of his ZR-15 smoking. "Never seen anything like these."

"Neither have I," Boggs said, setting the Plexiglas safety shield down before the poison could melt through and reach his skin.

"Powerful shit," Dagger said. "T-Bone's goggles were worthless."

Boggs reached for a metal sanitary can, and held up the shield quickly so the poison could drip into it.

"For the biologists," Boggs said. "They'll be here very soon."

Emoth groaned. "How long?" he asked.

Boggs collected the rest of the goo in the can. So far, the metal appeared to be holding as the slop bubbled and sizzled inside.

"Tomorrow," Boggs said.

Emoth shook his head. "They always muck things up," he said. "They get bossy, order us around, affect our safety."

Boggs carefully held the sanitary can and its deadly contents, then ran the onboard LifeForm scanner to see if any more of the creatures were waiting outside. All was clear.

For now.

Boggs flipped the laser bay switch, then strode down the bay ramp with the can and set it upon the ground.

"Dr. Tara will want that sample," he said.

Dagger and Emoth followed Boggs out onto Mawholla.

"Never heard of her," Emoth said. "I hope she's bringing a shovel so we can bury T-Bone. I hate when this shit happens. Makes me feel not human."

Boggs faced Emoth. "You're human," he said. "But you're also acting like a pussy. Take a look around you. What do you see?"

"It's getting dark," Emoth said.

"That's right," Boggs said. "This is not what we call *survival light*. Therefore, body retrieval is not in the cards for tonight, unless you want to strap on the night vision goggles, and then have them seared to your face forever from the spit of those things."

Dagger stepped forward, gripping his ZR-15. "And speaking of things," he said. "What do we call them, and why didn't the drones pick them up?"

"Who knows," Boggs said. "The drones haven't been reliable lately due to quality control. They're good, but not flawless. As for the creatures, I think 'Spitters' works for now. I'm sure Dr. Tara will have other ideas."

Dagger laughed sarcastically. "You know this woman, boss?"

Boggs sighed. His men were always fast to catch on. He'd had three dates with Dr. Tara back on Earth at the behest of friends and family, in an effort to begin the healing process over what happened to Sarah. The fact she worked as a biologist for CPB had been a complete coincidence. Things had gone well. They'd not had sex, only kissed, but he'd wanted a lot more. And he hated to admit it, but she kind of had his number. At first, it felt like he was betraying his deceased wife. But that faded on the third date, when Boggs realized he was still alive. He hadn't died, and he was done spending his nights alone between missions, empty beer cans strung about him.

Boggs turned to Dagger. "No," he said.

"Whatever you say boss," Dagger said.

4.

Boggs spent the night awake, observing the onboard LifeForm detector. Occasionally a bird flittered outside the ship, triggering a FRIENDLY alert from the LifeForm. Other creatures showed up, some similar to Earth marsupials, others reptilian in nature, but much smaller than the spitters. None of them were deemed dangerous by the LifeForm.

Boggs took a sip of his coffee spiked with adrenaline pills (AKA speed back on Earth) and clenched his fists. His men were right about T-Bone. It didn't feel human to not retrieve his remains, and bring them back to his family on Earth for a proper burial service. He hoped they would do that, but right now preservation of his crew, and continuing this mission was priority number one.

The onboard communications meter flashed, showing an image from the interior of the biologist's CAV-121. The crew was asleep in their Happy Boxes, while a timer flashed across the screen in red numbers: *ARRIVAL MAWHOLLA, T-minus 26 hours and 31 seconds*.

Boggs flicked off the screen. He felt like a creep watching them sleep, especially Dr. Tara.

Outside, the night creatures of Mawholla hummed and thrived. The LifeForm detector beeped again and again, but Boggs did not find what he had stayed up for.

The spitters knew better than to approach the ship after what happened to the one that had challenged Boggs. He had a hunch they were out there, waiting in the dark. And if Boggs strained hard enough at the monitors connected to external cameras, he swore he saw big, golf-ball sized eyes staring back at him in the darkness.

Boggs closed his eyes, and listened to his heart thudding thanks to his speed concoction. He wanted to sleep, but it was useless. He was, what he always was: a Shepherd watching over his flock.

5.

Boggs woke suddenly, the CAV alarms wailing at his side. Dagger, Portman, Emoth, and Staunch were behind him, flipping on the monitors.

"Wakey wakey time," Dagger said as he patted Boggs on the back. Boggs cleared the mental cobwebs from his mind.

"What time is it?" he asked.

"0400," Dagger said.

The main monitor flashed on, and Boggs wiped his sleep-deprived eyes to see better. As the external camera coasted around the CAV-117 on its track, numerous spitters loomed off in the woods, staring at them, waiting for their opportunity to pounce.

Staunch slammed his fist down on the console, his eyes beady and narrow. "What are we waiting for?" he said.

"They're lining up out there, waiting to be blasted by our outboard canons."

Boggs rubbed his thumb against his index finger, waiting patiently for the right moment to fire…or the right moment not to fire at all.

"Shit," Emoth said. "It's like shooting fish in a barrel right now. If I was in charge—"

"-but you're not in charge," Boggs said. "We have a directive from CPB on species annihilation."

Emoth ran his hands through his crew cut and stared at the monitors. "These fuckers killed T-Bone," he said. "We should wipe them out, like we wipe out other hostile species. I don't see what the fucking difference is here."

Boggs stood and faced Emoth. "I don't have to explain myself to you," he said. "But I will, because I want this to work. CPB wants it to work. The human race wants it to work. We have orders to defend ourselves, and to observe. We do not yet have orders to wipe out a species, like we've done before. The reason? Mawholla has a high probability of being The One. Get it? I've been doing this shit my entire life. Every planet has been a flop...like a chef flipping pancakes, or a fat guy diving into a pool. Too hot, too arid, not enough water, planets always on the edge of something, but never perfect and ripe in the middle, like Earth was, or like Mawholla is. There's no desert planet to contend with here, no oxygen scrubbers to engineer, no water replication system. In short, it is, by far the best option we've ever had. CPB knows what they're doing, and the biologists arriving here know it as well."

Boggs turned and pointed at the monitor. "You don't think I want to blow those things away after what they did to T-Bone? You don't think I want to blast every last one of them? I wouldn't feel bad about it, not for even one second. But I do feel bad about leaving T-Bone out there, and I'm sorry about that. But my job is to execute the missions while keeping as many of my men alive as possible."

"I agree," Portman said, addressing the other men. "The captain keeps a cool head, way cooler than most."

On the monitors, one of the spitters stepped from the ferns and approached the CAV.

"Great," Dagger said. "That might be the one that melted T-Bone's face off." Dagger turned and tried to hide his disappointment. "This sucks," he said. "It wasn't supposed to start out this way, this fast."

"Calm the fuck down," Portman said. "You're acting like a bitch."

"Fuck you," Dagger said, wiping the back of his hand against his lips.

"I'm serious," Portman said. "You're acting emotional and completely un-centered. This is not how a dominant male acts. A dominant male is indifferent and centered. You're all over the place, brother. Like a man who just got his first taste of pussy, and now he can't keep his shit together. Get it? Recon Elite Six is nothing BUT dominant males. Except for you. You're the emotional bitch."

Dagger set his gun down, and swung at Portman. Portman ducked, and delivered an uppercut blow to Dagger's jaw. Dagger cried out with a puzzled look on his face, and stumbled backwards.

Boggs leapt from the monitor area and seized Dagger before he could smash his head onto a metal support beam.

"Alright," Boggs said. "That's enough bullshit. The next man who gets physical within the group will feel my wrath. Got it?"

"Yes sir!" the men shouted back, sans Dagger, who was knocked clean cold from Portman's blow.

"And you," Boggs said to Portman. "Come on, man. You know you have the upper hand with him. Control yourself in situations like that."

"Yes sir," Portman said. "I just wanted to have your back, sir."

Boggs nodded. "I appreciate that," he said. "But not to the detriment of core morale. I can keep our men in line, on my own. Been doing it for years. I'm asking you to have my back, but also to keep your shit together."

Boggs turned and faced the group. "No more of this," he said. "No more. We work as a team, and that means having each other's backs physically, and psychologically. Am I clear?"

"Yes sir!" the group said.

"Good. Now fire the god damn canons on the spitter that made the mistake of leaving the forest to approach the CAV."

"Oh hell yes," Staunch said. He manipulated the analog joystick until the canon markers were upon the spitter, whose eyes widened as the canon motors whirred quietly outside.

Staunch thumbed the fire button, and the spitter jiggled like a puppet whose master had way too much caffeine. Then it slumped to the ground, blood oozing out its mouth and eyes.

"Goodnight Irene," Staunch said.

Dagger awoke, and wobbled to his feet. "Oh hell yes," he said, his hand rubbing his jaw. "Payback sucks."

Dagger turned to Portman and slapped him on the shoulder. "And nice shot, man. I deserved it."

Portman returned the shoulder slap. "No worries, man." Then he reached out his hand. "I'm sorry I did it."

Dagger shook Portman's hand. "Don't be. I'm just glad we were able to take care of a spitter. I hope it's the one that got T-Bone."

"I doubt it," Boggs said.

Staunch took a sip from his hydration unit, and pointed at the monitor. "Wait a second," he said. "Something's moving out there."

Boggs checked the monitor. Staunch was right. Something was moving out there, but this seemed much larger than the spitters they'd seen before. And "much larger" was a pathetic way of putting it. The thing looked like the smaller spitters, from what Boggs could tell. But all he could see of it was its lower legs, and the python-like tail as it hurled itself towards the CAV.

"Fire," Boggs said.

Staunch laid onto the external canon, firing dozens of rounds at the creature's legs and tail.

But the thing still kept coming.

"Jesus," Dagger said.

The CAV-117 rocked to the side as the giant spitter collided with the frame.

Boggs fought off the shakiness, and slammed his fist down on the Shell Shock button. A second later, a static surge buzzed through the CAV shell as the outer hull electrified itself for its own self-defense. The giant spitter wailed, and retreated towards the woods.

"Hit it," Boggs ordered.

Staunch fired the canon repeatedly into the thing's tail, tearing off chunks of flesh. It ran off into the woods, its angry roars coming loud and clear through the cabin's speakers.

"What the hell was that thing?" Emoth asked.

"The big momma," Portman said. "When you piss enough of 'em off, they send her."

Boggs let out a deep sigh. It had been one hell of a 24-hour period. "Probably," he said. "The spitters seem very intelligent. They exhibit pack behavior, and have a dominant leader. The big momma obviously fills that role."

Dagger stared at the woods through the console's 56 inch monitor and shook his head. "How do we engage something of that size out there, without the protection of the CAV?" he said.

"Good question," Boggs said. "But we do have a special weapon for this mission thanks to the folks at CPB."

Boggs walked over to a metal locker cell, and punched in a code onto a keypad that was fastened to the door. The locker clicked open, and Boggs removed a hefty bazooka-like device, except slightly more compact, leading to a small white rectangular pack. He shouldered the weapon, then patted the barrel. "Gentlemen, meet the Havoc 12."

"Sweet," Dagger said. "A bazooka. I'm not sure it will do much against the big momma."

Boggs grinned. "Is that what you think? Because men, the rounds that a Havoc 12 releases can tear through a population of big mommas."

The men looked on, incredulous.

"How's that?" Emoth asked.

"One round can cut through a hundred men," Boggs said. "The Havoc 12 rounds are heat-seeking, with titanium reinforced tips. On top of that, you curious cats, the rounds are rocket propelled, meaning the gift of death just keeps on giving and giving."

"Damn," Dagger said. "How does that round not kill us?"

"The Havoc 12 is programmed to ignore the heat signature of the human body, combined with a quick brain scan of the target upon firing. We have really big brains. The spitters do not, so far as we can tell. Nor do some of the lizard-like species we've been fighting on other planets."

"How many rounds can it fire?"

"One," Boggs said, as he held up a huge bullet. "Until we propel this from the base unit I'm holding right now, you cannot load another. The potential for collateral damage and complete chaos is just too high."

Emoth sniffed the air like a dog, and smiled. "You smell that fellas?" he said. "That's the smell of death. For them."

Dagger grinned. "And then we can go get T-Bone."

Boggs frowned. "I wish that more than anything," he said. "But it's likely the spitters, or some other species has fed on him."

"Jesus," Dagger said. "I knew we should've grabbed him right there."

"We'd be dead," Staunch said. "And likely eaten too."

Boggs set the Havoc 12 back into the locker, and closed it shut. "When the suns come up this morning, we'll go check on T-Bone, see if we can get him back. But we're bringing the Havoc 12 with us, just in case big momma decides to make another appearance."

"Good," Dagger said.

6.

The two suns rose above Mawholla's 16,000 foot mountains, lighting up the forest and meadows in serene light.

Boggs turned off the interlaced lasers, and headed down the ramp with his men. On his shoulder he carried the Havoc 12. He checked the waste can in which he'd kept the spitter slime, and was saddened to see the saliva had eaten through the can and spread out evenly in the dirt. Whatever active ingredients had been in the saliva, were no longer active. Boggs wondered about the power of dirt and sand to neutralize the acidity, and he made a mental note.

The ancient forest loomed on their east, west, and south. To the north, rose the meadow where they'd seen the injured moose-like animal.

"Is Recon Elite Six ready?" Boggs asked.

"Yes sir," the men said.

"Okay," Boggs said. "It's go time."

Boggs stepped into the meadow, aiming the Havoc 12 as he walked, while Emoth and Portman had his six.

"They were all over our shit last night," Dagger said. "I bet they're hiding, just waiting for us to stumble into the woods. Then they'll pounce, and spit. And melt our fuckin brains off."

Portman sighed. "Dagger," he said.

"Yeah?" Dagger said.

"Shut the fuck up."

Dagger frowned, but proceeded ahead, just behind Boggs.

Clouds covered the two suns, and whatever light there'd been, became not so much.

Boggs stepped into the woods. Each crunch of his boot made him wince. He tried to avoid the leaves and sticks, but they crunched and snapped like devious minions set to betray him and his men.

"Damn leaves are everywhere," Staunch said as he hawked a ball of spit onto a branch.

"We need to clear the meadow-bordering forest," Boggs said.

"And see what we can see."

After hiking for a while, and dodging deadfalls and bus-sized logs, they came upon the area where T-Bone's body should've been.

"Shit," Dagger said, pointing to a patch of compressed ferns. "This is where he was. Right fucking here."

Boggs sighed as he observed bits of brain and other human tissue sticking to leaves. He turned on his LifeForm meter after setting down the Havoc 12 and dialed in T-Bone's 4 digit tracking code.

The signal beeped green, fifty yards into the brush.

Boggs put his finger to his lips in a "shushing" motion, and turned to his men. Then he turned down the annoying beeping from the LifeForm, and stepped as carefully as he could into the forest, handing off the LifeForm to Portman, while he slung the Havoc 12 back over his shoulder.

The men crept closer to the beeping, which at this point seemed absolutely static in nature.

Or so they thought.

After passing a huge fallen log lit up by several enormous sun rays punching through the canopy, they came upon a clearing.Boggs parted aside head-high ferns, and took a look.

A spitter lay bedded in a patch of grass, licking blood and other tissue from its front claws.

Damn, Boggs thought.

Further examination of the scene revealed a human skeleton lying twisted in a heap just feet from the bathing spitter. Shreds of skin lay attached to the bone here and there, and an eyeball hung loosely from the skull socket by a lone thread of sinew.

It was clear T-Bone's tracking tag had been consumed by the spitter.

Behind Boggs, Emoth stepped on a branch way too loud, sending a sick CRACK into the woods.

The spitter stood and glared at the men with the yellow almond eyes of a snake.

Boggs wished they'd had better goggles. Way better. But he wondered if T-Bone would've still died regardless of the quality. The venom was ridiculously corrosive.

The spitter hissed, and a second later three more spitters emerged from behind the first. To Bogg's dismay, the hidden spitters had simply been bedded down behind the initial spitter, quiet as mice.

Boggs wished they were mice.

And of course, they charged.

Boggs held a hand up to make sure his men held their fire, then brought his hand back to steady the Havoc 12. He pressed the trigger, and a hollow THUD echoed across the forest. A computer beeped twice on the onboard Havoc 12 digital display, capturing the heat signatures of the intended targets.

The round emerged from the barrel almost in slow motion, propelled by a new breed of propulsion technology. It bore a hole into the first spitter's heart, and the beast clutched at what was left of its chest before gasping into death. The three other spitters reared back and let loose their deadly saliva, splattering the trees and knocking the Havoc 12 round off course.

"Shit," Dagger said. "They're fucking spitting."

Portman gripped his ZR-15 and spat. "Uh yeah, that's what they do."

Boggs felt a bit of saliva sting his right cheek, like the mother of all wasps had gotten him. He set the Havoc 12 down and swapped the crap from his face, feeling lucky to be wearing gloves.

Things had not gone so well for Emoth. A gob of spitter's venom had landed on his right shoulder, and started to eat its way through his camo uniform. He screamed as the venom burned and froze him simultaneously.

Meanwhile, the Havoc 12 round met its second target, blowing through the spitter's right eye and exiting out its brain, before hitting a 90 degree angle and entering the next spitter at its belly, just above the left lower leg. The spitter collapsed and screeched, spitting up venom into the air. Boggs grabbed Emoth and shielded him from the spray, letting it pepper his own uniform. A moment later Boggs felt the sting of a thousand wasps. Behind him, the Havoc 12 round exited the third spitter, and then proceeded to crush the next spitter's right leg, blowing through bone and sinew.

Dagger, Staunch, and Portman were on it, firing their ZR-15s as they finished off the wounded spitters.

But there was no time for Boggs to rejoice in their small victory. He was in pain, really, serious pain, and so was Emoth. He mustered whatever strength he could and got to his feet, while holding Emoth under his arm as Portman grabbed the other.

"Back to the ship," Boggs said. "He needs medical attention."

"So do you sir," Dagger said.

Boggs said nothing.

The men hurried back through Mawholla's old growth forest as the Havoc 12 round zig-zagged through the trees behind them. Boggs heard another spitter cry out in agony, and then the Havoc 12 round finally sputtered out and screamed high into the sky before self-detonating. This was a programmed feature to protect those who fired the weapon.

Studies had indicated the Havoc 12 had a 99% non-friendly fire accident rate. But there was still that 1%, which was never far from Boggs' mind whenever he slung the Havoc 12 over his shoulder.

Boggs stumbled as he helped carry Emoth. But was it his own doing, or had something made him stumble?

There, yet again, the ground was shaking.

A skin-crawling roar echoed across the forest, and at that moment Boggs knew without a doubt a big momma had been alerted to their presence.

"Go go go" he said, trying his best to ignore the stinging on his back.

"Fuck," Dagger said. "The big momma. I can feel her thumping the ground. Fuck fuck fuck."

The men entered the meadow and lurched forward as fast as they could muster. Boggs turned briefly to look behind him, and saw the canopy parting as a big momma tore after them.

The CAV-117 appeared fifty yards ahead, just as a dozen smaller spitters appeared from the tree line behind them. Boggs turned and hoofed it as the spitters reared back and let their saliva fly. Heaps of it zinged past Boggs and his men, landing in the meadow grass and sizzling.

His men deftly made sure to miss as much of it as they could, and reached the bay ramp.

With spit raining down on the CAV, they hurled themselves up the ramp. Portman slammed the button, sealing them off from their pursuers. Boggs flicked on the main console monitor, and watched as big momma emerged from the forest, heading straight for the CAV.

"Time for someone to learn a lesson," Boggs said. He slammed his fist down on a button, and the ship shield activated. But instead of big momma ramming into the ship, the huge spitter stopped in the middle of the meadow, tilting its head curiously as the ship hummed.

"Fuck, they're learning," Dagger said.

"Say it ain't so," Staunch said as he helped Emoth out of his clothes and into a Life Chamber in the ship's medical bay. Once Emoth was tucked into the chamber, Staunch closed the lid and activated the unit.

On the main console, Boggs and the others watched as big momma and a herd of smaller spitters waited patiently in the meadow.

"Let's see just how much," Boggs said. He maneuvered the external canon joystick, just to get the motor track running.Outside, the spitters recognized the noise, and returned to the tree line, where they were partially-hidden in the thick vegetation.

"Well I'll be," Portman said as he stretched on a pair of gloves, and stuffed Emoth's contaminated clothing into a waste disposal receptacle. "They learn fast."

"Faster than anything I've seen," Boggs said. "But still not as smart as us."

Dagger chuckled. "Oh really?" he said. "Maybe they're smarter. Maybe they aren't dumb enough to fuck up their own planet with pollution and overpopulation, and need to build shit to get off that planet."

Boggs turned to Dagger. "Choose your words very carefully," he said, wincing at what felt like dozens of wasp stings along his back and shoulders.

Portman pointed at Boggs. "You need to get out of those clothes," he said. "I can smell that shit, smells like a Twinkie that's been left in a freezer for a year."

"I hate Twinkies," Boggs said as he carefully stripped out of his clothing, and tossed them in the receptacle bin. "Take charge of the external controls," he said to Staunch, before opening up a Life Chamber and laying down inside. Portman pressed a button along the side, and the bubble lid closed over Boggs. He closed his eyes, aching for the stinging and itching on his back to go away. Soon he heard a soft beep, and the whirring of oxygen flooding the chamber.

"Good morning," a robotic female voice said through tiny speakers.

"I've been hit with some kind of acidic poison from a hostile life form," Boggs said to the computer.

"I see," the voice said. "We have not treated this kind of wound before. However, I am running a log to see potential treatments."

The cool oxygen fanned across Boggs' body, and he opened his eyes to see his men watching over the main console, and the spitters partially-hidden in the tree line.

A moment later, he felt a pleasant sensation on his backside, as numerous vents in the padding released painkillers, or some kind of soothing treatment. He sighed, and the female voice came to him again:

"How's that feeling?" the computer asked.

"Better," Boggs said.

"I assumed that would be the response," the computer said. "I've created hybrid pain relief and antibacterial aerosol mist, which should clean and relieve the wounds."

The computer paused for thirty seconds. "Are you still feeling positive reactions to this treatment?" it then said.

"Yes," Boggs said. "Like new."

The computer voice paused. "You are not new, Captain Boggs. You are 43 years old."

"I'm in better shape than most guys half my age," Boggs said.

"Hold on while I check my records," the computer voice said.

Boggs sighed. Oh how he hated tight spaces.

"Yes, what you say is correct," the computer said. "You are in better physical condition than 73.59 percent of men half your age, as per the CPB medical database."

"Like I said," Boggs said.

Boggs reached for the inside lever, to flip the bubble glass open so he could rejoin his men.

"I'm afraid you have five minutes left," the computer said. "Abating treatment at this point will increase odds for the need of further treatment. Remember, the best medicine is not band-aid medicine, Captain. It is preventive medicine."

Boggs laid back down and sighed. But he also grinned for a moment, too. Because not only was he not feeling the wasp sting of the poison anymore, but he also wasn't feeling much of anything else, either. The aches and pains from years of service to CPB faded. So did the pain of losing Sarah and Connor. Great feelings of euphoria overcame him. He felt like everything was absolutely perfect in the universe, and he had a desire to be everyone's best friend.

The computer voice chimed in. "Adverse side effects of tropo-pain medication are feelings of grandiosity and euphoria, along with constipation, Captain. Judgment is often impaired. Please refrain from dangerous activity and decision making for one-half hour after administration."

"Thanks for the heads up," Boggs said.

"You're welcome," the computer said. "It is my directive to keep the crew healthy and safe."

Boggs opened one eye, and watched his men watching the center console.

He would've loved an open order to wipe these things out. Maybe that was coming soon.

Maybe.

7.

Boggs arose from his treatment and felt a slight head rush. Other than that, he felt noticeably better. There were still a few itches, but the pain was gone. He checked the monitor along with his crew, and turned to Emoth, who lay asleep in his Life Chamber.

The cool AC inside the bay brushed against Boggs' healing skin as he asked Emoth's Life Chamber for a status update. A 10 inch screen on the outside of the chamber revealed that Emoth was at 60% health, with an "unknown" substance infecting his body. He was being given a course of Rocephin antibiotic, delivered in aerosol format. Apparently the poison had entered his body cavity, and was reeking all kinds of havoc. His heart monitor showed irregular beats as his body battled.

Boggs sighed.

He had the distinct sensation he wasn't leading his men properly. However, he had to be fair to himself. The spitters were not the slow, mangy desert animals they'd encountered before, nor the easily avoided bacteria on the ice planets they'd been ordered to scout. These animals were much bigger, and much more dangerous. Not to mention Mawholla's forest ecosystem provided significant cover. Boggs scanned his mind, thumbing through his history lessons back on planet Earth. There had been a war in the 1970's called Vietnam. Americans had lost the war, and the real reason for the loss was the ecosystem. It had been a major hurdle to victory. And Boggs guessed that was the kind of thing he and his men had here. It wasn't just about the spitters. And if the biologists gave the go ahead, they'd be required to begin the process of wiping out the species so humans could colonize the planet. More than anything, the continued survival of the human species took precedent. There was no question as to his directive. And if that meant killing off an entire species, he'd do it. If it meant sacrificing his men to get the job done, he'd do that too. The sum was greater than its parts. If they were meant to be a sacrificial spearhead to continue the human race, so be it. The funny thing was, Boggs *liked* it. He felt himself and his men running parallel with other historical figures like Lewis and Clark. It was his job to pave the way for the rest.

Staunch turned to him, a concerned look on his face. "What now boss?" he asked.

Boggs thought about it for a second.

"We hunker down until CAV-121 arrives," he said. "We'll confer with the biologists."

"You mean your girlfriend," Dagger said.

Boggs went to explain, then thought better of it. Explaining too much would make him look weak in front of his men. Instead, he ignored Dagger and focused his attention back on Emoth.

The LCD readout indicated Emoth's pulse was beating at 40 BPM, and getting slower by the minute. Through the glass, Boggs watched as Emoth seized out, arms forced to his sides as his legs kicked. Whatever was in him was killing him.

Soon the rest of the crew huddled around Emoth's chamber, except for Staunch, who had his thumb on the canon joystick, and his eyes on the monitors.

Emoth began to shake harder and harder, his legs hitting the protective plastic of his bubble.

"Jesus," Dagger said, "isn't there something we can do?"

Boggs put his hand on Dagger's shoulder. "There's nothing we can do at this point," Boggs said. "It's up to the Life Chamber computer medics."

"We have doctors flying in tomorrow," Dagger said.

"A medic, and several biologists," Boggs said. "Myself, and the CPB have put our faith in these devices numerous times, with higher recovery rates than human-conducted medicine. You have to trust the chambers, and me."

Dagger clenched his fist around his ZR-15.

"And you can put that down now, too," Boggs said. "There are no spitters in here."

The men watched helplessly as Emoth seized and spasmed. The Life Chamber lights flashed, and emitted aerosol mists to treat whatever that vile shit was inside of him.

"It's got his heart," Portman said. "Imagine that shit being in your heart."

Through the protective plastic bubble, Emoth screamed again and again while kicking his legs and thumping the plastic.

But something else was thumping. Powerful steps came from outside the CAV, and the entire craft shook and rumbled.

"Big momma has arrived," Staunch said. "She must've jumped from somewhere, because I didn't get a whiff of her."

Boggs slammed the external electrifying switch, and watched as Big Momma sprinted across the meadow away from the ship.

"Ha!" Dagger said. "That will teach her."

But Boggs didn't feel quite right. Something was off. "Hold up," he said.

The men waited patiently in front of the monitors, eyes scanning for any kind of movement.

As Emoth pounded on the bubble lid of his Life Chamber, something else pounded the ground, to the point the CAV shook as if in an earthquake.

And then Boggs saw it. Or them.

A half-dozen big mommas raced towards the CAV. Staunch thumbed the canon joystick and fired, plugging the creature's knees and legs full of lead. But it did not stop the initial impact. The big mommas were just too many.

Boggs reached out for a support beam as the men and gear flew across the bay. To Boggs' horror, the CAV rocked up to one side, even as he could smell the burning flesh of the big mommas as the electrical defenses fried their skin.

Boggs felt like he'd been punched in the head. Emoth spasmed against the bubble lid now, instead of resting flat inside the Life Chamber. His other men tumbled to portside, grasping for anything they could to keep from smashing their heads against the console units. Jolts of electricity rocked the exterior of the CAV as the spitters shrieked in pain. Yet despite it all, Boggs could see the big mommas working as a team on the external cameras to flip the CAV over.

Boggs sighed and grimaced.

He'd miscalculated the spitter's ingenuity, and now he and his men were going to pay a very dear price for that miscalculation.

Another big momma raced towards the CAV and impacted with tremendous force. It let out a painful roar as the CAV teetered on the brink of flipping over.

"We've gotta get the fuck out of here," Dagger said as he held on for his life.

The stench of frying flesh and the roaring big mommas intensified. Boggs was extremely glad he'd put the Havoc 12 back in its proper storage locker. What he wasn't glad about was Emoth, who'd become unresponsive after all that spasming.

Boggs struggled in the upheaval to reach for the voice COMMS switch. A tablet smacked into his arm, and he winced at the pain.

"Fuck this," Staunch said. "These things are going to kill us."

"Shut your mouth," Boggs said, as he was finally able to muster the strength to hit the blue switch. When he did, he spoke firmly and immediately to the ship computer. "Danni," he said, "commence take off and evasive maneuvers."

The COMM voice spoke back, at first distorting through the ship's speakers as the big mommas wreaked havoc. "Yes Captain," Danni said. "Commencing take off".

The ship's engines whirred to life, causing the big mommas to pause. The ship righted itself with a tremendous thud, sending Boggs and his men flying.

Boggs held his head and braced for impact.

CRUNCH!

Portman slammed into a column support and grunted. The CAV jolted again, but this time the movement was caused by Danni and the propulsion engines. Slowly they rose, and Boggs watched as two big mommas held on.

"Danni, proceed to three thousand feet above current position," Boggs said.

Danni obliged, and the CAV rose steadily above Mawholla. Boggs checked the external cameras, and saw two big mommas clinging on for dear life.

"Oh hell yes," Dagger said. "Somebody's going for a nice little drop."

Boggs' stomach churned as the CAV rose faster and faster.

"We've reached 3,000 feet, Captain," Danni said.

"Good," Boggs said.

As the big momma's feet dangled from the craft, Boggs took hold of the canon joystick and began hammering them, sending chunks of skin and bone flying through the sky. The jumbo spitters roared, then let go, their claws making horrible scraping sounds as they slipped down the CAV.

"Woohoo fuckers!" Dagger said as the men watched the spitters tumble towards certain death on Mawholla.

"That's for T-Bone and Emoth," Dagger said. "Ain't so smart now, eh?"

With the CAV stable, Boggs checked on Emoth.

He was dead.

"Help me get him to the preservation chamber," Boggs said.

Portman, Staunch, and Dagger stared at Emoth, saying nothing.

"Come on," Boggs said as he punched in the access code for Emoth's Life Chamber. He took Emoth by the shoulders, while Staunch took him by the feet.

"It didn't have to be like this," Portman said. "Two men already? Shit."

"It's a new planet," Boggs said. "And despite what happened to T-Bone and Emoth, it's a livable planet...the best chance we have."

"I wish we were back on Stygis, shooting lizards the size of iguanas," Dagger said.

Boggs frowned at Dagger. "Wishing is for cowards," Boggs said. "Men make use of the current moment."

A few minutes later, Emoth's body was placed in a preservation chamber and sealed inside.

Boggs headed back to the main cabin, keeping his cool despite everything that had happened. This was his job. "Danni," he said, "I need to speak with Dr. Tara and the incoming biologists."

"Captain, the crew on the CAV-121 are all in their Happy Boxes," Danni said.

Shit, Boggs thought. He should've known better.

"Danni," Boggs said, "Ship damage report, immediately."

"Yes Captain," Danni said. "Please wait while I run the diagnostics."

Boggs waited, as Portman and Staunch walked up behind him.

He was losing his patience with the computers and the spitters, at least temporarily. He'd had ship damage many times before, but usually caused by weather conditions, NOT life forms the size of Earth dinosaurs.

"I'm afraid the external shields have been damaged 52%," Danni said. "The CAV, at this time, is unable to leave the atmosphere without on-board casualties."

Boggs balled his fingers into a fist and tried his best not to punch the wall. He'd had a feeling things would be that bad. The big mommas must have torn the shit out of the heat shingles.

"Great," Dagger said. "Stuck on this shithole?"

Boggs turned to Dagger. "For now," he said, turning to address the rest of his men. "But don't let it affect your morale. Remember, Dagger, we're MOVING here. And a good chunk of our planet as soon as we can. Would you rather be stuck on our dying planet, or stuck on the planet we're supposed to move to?"

Boggs watched Dagger think about it for a few seconds, his eyes searching the cabin for his thoughts.

"There's no one here but us," Dagger said, looking young, maybe too young. "I'd rather die with my family, on a planet I know."

Staunch stepped in and placed his hand on Dagger's shoulder. He made direct, firm eye contact with him, in an understanding sort of way. "I get it," he said. "You're having a hard time with this. Planet Strober was a desert planet without much action. You didn't break in the way you should've."

Dagger looked terrified. "It was still a big deal to me," he said. "I'd never been off Earth."

Boggs kept his fist balled, and wondered how Dagger had passed the psychological profile for Recon Elite Six.

"Look," Staunch said. "I need you to be tougher. We all need you to be tougher. Can you do that for me? For us?"

Dagger looked around the cabin, and at the consoles that showed thick, rain-filled clouds above Mawholla, and the ship's own exhaust ports distorting the air.

"I can," Dagger said. "I will. I'll do better."

Staunch slapped him on the shoulder. "That's my boy," he said.

Boggs interrupted the men, and spoke to Danni. "Danni," he said, "please configure a new landing area."

Dagger looked like someone had taken a piano off his back.

"Are you sure, Captain?" Danni asked.

"Yes," Boggs said. "We're not going back down to that meadow."

8.

The damaged CAV flew across Mawholla. Boggs made sure that Danni had sent communications to the biologists' CAV, with an update on their location change. The communication would be encrypted and stored in a hyper-lock software drive, and played back as Priority One when the crew awoke from their Happy Boxes.

As the CAV flew, Boggs had the onboard computers run extended diagnostic scans on the planet. The CAV was much more powerful than the drones initially sent to Mawholla. In a half hour, readouts from the scan results flashed across a side monitor.

Boggs shook his head. More of the same, basically. The planet was two thirds land, one third ocean. Almost all of the land was of the type of forest ecosystem, except for two large meadow-like areas at the south and north poles. Boggs realized these were Arctic tundra, with big ice sheets occupying half of the meadow areas.

The planet was the best candidate ever assessed by CPB. There was simply nothing in the same league. Boggs felt proud of his crew, and CPB (despite them being a pain in the ass at times). But he felt other things, also. Unsettling things. He'd lost two men. Two good men.

"Danni," Boggs said as he sipped a warm mug of instant coffee. "Chart a course for the northern tundra meadow."

"Yes Captain," Danni said.

Dagger came up from behind Boggs. "Where are we headed?" he asked.

"To an open area," Boggs said. "We'll have much better sightlines."

Dagger looked confused.

"I thought our job was to get rid of hostile species," Dagger said.

Boggs nodded. "That's correct. If that species is deemed too dangerous to co-habitat with."

"Then what are we waiting for, sir?"

"The biologists," Boggs said. "Before we kill off any species, we need to learn if they can be beneficial to us in some way. Or, we need to learn if killing them off will disrupt a natural balance, that in turn might affect us negatively."

Dagger nodded. "I get it," he said.

"I know you do, son. Basically, we are the bull. Lock, stock and barrel. But we can't be the bull in a china shop."

Boggs sipped his coffee, as Staunch and Portman met him in front of the monitors.

"Looks good," Staunch said as he eyed the meadow-like terrain unfolding before them. "Temps the same?"

"Slightly cooler," Boggs said. "Like our Arctic in summer."

Portman tore into a silver pouch of veggie protein. "Despite what's happened to us, I'm conflicted," he said. "I feel like…I feel like it could be home. But I also feel like it might be the end of us. I'm not sure we have a choice."

"I get the same," Boggs said. "We have our work cut out for us."

"I'll third that," Staunch said. "We gotta go somewhere. And Mawholla beats the shit out of the other planets. It's not even close."

Staunch raised an eyebrow. "Has the scanner picked up new life forms?" he asked.

"Yes," Boggs said. "More moose-like animals, and numerous bird and fish species. Most of them deemed harmless, and many deemed useful for sustenance purposes."

"Mmm…fish," Portman said as he flexed his huge bicep. "I like cod."

Boggs nodded. "Our oceans back home are just about out of that, aren't they?"

"Not just," Portman said. "Are."

Boggs popped on Level 3 of the scanner, which quickly streamed on the third side monitor. Schools upon schools of shimmering, vibrant fish swam in a deep blue ocean that reminded Boggs of the northern Atlantic. "There's enough to go around for everyone," he said.

But as soon as he said it, he regretted it. As he'd spent more and more time on Mawholla, a certain ominous feeling had begun to creep up on him and weigh heavy in his thoughts. All of the pristine landscapes: the mountains, the old growth forest, the untouched rivers and the flourishing wildlife had made him think bad thoughts. For the first time in his life, ever, he'd felt like a parasite. The bad guy. The-one-who-should-not-be-here. He felt the totality of the universe in every pore of his skin. And perhaps, he was now finally feeling the inevitability, that perhaps humankind was meant to die with Earth. For after all, wasn't it humankind that had gone terribly wrong and killed its own mother Earth?

Boggs frowned.

How would they change? If anything, the human race had proven they'd repeat the same mistakes over and over again. The only thing potentially saving their asses this time was their knack for technology.

And here they were, looking for a new mother.

"Sir," Dagger said. "You alright?"

Boggs shook out the mental cobwebs and stood. "Yeah," he said. "Just going over some of our planning."

A lie, certainly, but a pivot to the truth.

"We're going to get our boots wet in this northern meadow area," he said. "We've already established that the forested and mountainous continent known as Morina is probably full of spitters based on the consistent habitat-type. We need to establish if this new ecosystem also holds hostile species."

"Yes sir," Dagger said.

For the first time, Boggs sensed confidence in Dagger. Maybe the time in service was building on him, hardening him. He hoped so.

Dagger mimicked Boggs by drinking his coffee black, and from a similar mug.

Boggs turned back to the main console. "Danni, set us down in a stable environment in quadrant 39."

"Yes Captain," Danni said. "The ecosystem here presents a challenge. I'm detecting numerous burrow-structures beneath the tundra. I would advise upmost caution when vacating the CAV."

Boggs nodded. "Noted," he said.

Dagger sipped his coffee as he stared out the cabin window. "Will you be bringing the Havoc 12?" he asked Boggs.

Boggs turned to Dagger, grinning from ear to ear.

"You bet your ass," Boggs said.

9.

The men stepped onto the tundra as Boggs slung the Havoc 12 over his shoulder. The ground sunk beneath his boots an inch or so, and Boggs could feel the watery instability as he took several more steps.

Portman frowned. "Sucks you down," he said.

"It's not too bad," Dagger said as he lit up a cigarette.

Boggs shook his head. "Come on man, really?"

Dagger looked sheepish. "Can't help it sir," he said. "My dad got me started young on the farm."

"It's fine. For now," Boggs said. "We have bigger fish to fry."

Dagger exhaled, and let loose his pollution into the pristine Mawholla sky. "I hope there's no fucking spitters up this way," he said.

"Well," Boggs said, "you have the LifeForm meter. I have an unfortunate feeling we're going to need it."

Dagger snubbed out his cigarette and pocketed the filter, then did as ordered.

Boggs nodded at Portman, who followed Dagger's lead-which made Boggs warm inside.

Dagger led the way, LifeForm meter held out, while Staunch and Boggs brought up the rear, weapons aimed.

Boggs was glad for his Sola-Tech waterproof boots and gaiters. The combo didn't let any of the water in, although he could feel just how damn cold the water was, like stepping into liquid ice cubes. The air smelled impossibly pristine, with a whiff of decaying grass and moist soil.

A flock of birds flew high overhead, and Boggs could tell they were small and harmless, perhaps rustled up by the commotion the CAV made upon landing.

Staunch licked his lips. "I bet them birds just fled their nests," he said. "We could cook us up some Mawholla scrambled eggs," he said.

"Another time," Boggs said.

"I know that," Staunch said. "Just sayin'."

Boggs sunk down even lower this time, his pant leg feeling the full chill of the water. Dagger and Portman had veered left, and he should've too.

"Watch your step, sir," Dagger said ahead of him.

For a moment, Boggs felt the ground move.

Or maybe it was just post-nerve movement from flying in the CAV.

There, yet again.

Great, Boggs thought. *Earthquake.*

But was it? Boggs wondered.

"Sir," Dagger said as his LifeForm beeped. "I'm getting a dangerous reading on a very large animal. But it's coming not ahead of us, but BENEATH us."

The ground quaked and lurched beneath Boggs' boots, as water bubbles percolated to the surface, and broke repeatedly. Then Boggs watched as chunks of sod and soil tented in front of him.

"Split apart, step back, facing each other at north, south, west, and east," Boggs said. "Not too fast, not too slow."

What was left of Recon Elite Six followed their captain's orders. It was hard for Boggs to watch events unfold as Dagger and Portman's LifeForm meters roared to life with danger readings.

The ground heaved again. Whatever it was, was coming up. Whether they liked it or not.

At last the thing broke through, mounds of dirt and water gushing off of its…face. If Boggs could even call it that. It reminded Boggs of a giant earthworm, complete with ringed sections.

Except for two, not-so-tiny details.

This worm had to be at least thirty feet long, and ten feet thick. And when it opened its bizarre, hidden mouth, it spit venom, just like the spitters.

The first shot missed Portman.

Staunch opened fire with his ZR-15 as the creature roared. Chunks of weird worm flesh peppered the air, and the thing appeared to bleed Neosporin.

The worm shot its venom again, and Boggs ducked the phlegmy mass as it plopped into the moist grass and sizzled at his feet.

By now, Dagger and Portman had pocketed their LifeForms, and were reaching for their weapons.

"Obliterate," Boggs said as he set down the Havoc 12 and aimed his ZR-15.

The sound of gunfire and madness filled the tundra as the worm spat repeatedly into the air. Boggs and his men dodged the falling venom, then resumed firing, hacking apart the worm.

And boy, was it getting hacked. Hundreds upon hundreds of gaping flesh wounds seeped the Neosporin-looking fluid as they continued to fire. Boggs had to wonder what the hell it would take to kill the thing. A thousand rounds?

He thought about ending it all and using the Havoc 12. One of their directives was to have a minimalistic impact on Mawholla, in anything they did. This was some full-on Rambo shit.

Before Boggs could finish his thought, the shredded worm collapsed to Mawholla, and groaned several raspy breaths before falling silent.

As the last rifle shots faded, silence reclaimed Mawholla. The men stared at the enormous creature they'd just destroyed.

"What the fuck is this thing?" Dagger asked.

"Some kind of burrowing species," Boggs said. "I was informed of the possibility due to Mawholla's rich soil. But I never imagined this size."

Staunch walked up to the beast and gave it a good kick with his boot. "Serves it right," he said.

"I don't think 'right' has anything to do with it," Boggs said. "It's just a worm."

Portman patted the beast with a gloved hand.

"Don't touch it," Boggs said. "We don't know-"

Before Boggs could finish, something strange happened. One of the wounds that leaked the Neosporin substance squeaked.

"What the fuck was that?" Dagger asked, pointing his rifle at the wound.

"Get back Portman," Boggs said.

Portman stumbled backwards in the sinking tundra just as a creature slopped forth from the gaping wound. It scurried towards Portman as he wildly fired numerous shots.

None of which hit the creature.

"Parasites," Boggs said.

Boggs took Dagger's LifeForm meter and thumbed it on. It flashed the danger sign repeatedly.

The creature, with a drill-shaped head, eight legs, and the tail of a rat squeaked and snickered as it tried to chew into Portman's boot. Portman found his footing, and kicked it hard. The creature went flying and splashed into a puddle.

The men stood there, watching and waiting, hands wrapped around their ZR-15s.

The creature rose on hind legs and sniffed the air. Then it let loose a cry.

Uh-oh, Boggs thought.

The parasite clicked two front legs (or arms…whatever the hell they were) and glanced backwards. The giant worm's flesh quivered where the rifle wounds ran with clear fluid. The head of another parasite emerged from the flesh, and then another. Soon, twenty parasites plopped out of the worm's wounds, and clacked and clicked their way towards Recon Elite Six.

Portman's LifeForm beeped repeatedly.

"Says they're dangerous," Portman said.

"Well," Boggs said, a sarcastic grin spreading across his face. "Take them out."

Dagger and Staunch opened fire, shooting up a combo of ice water, soil, and guts as the rounds decimated the parasites and whatever was behind them.

Boggs made sure to help out, picking off three or four parasites with his ZR-15.

The original parasite stood, then let out a whistle pig cry, and fled the scene along with the remaining parasites, some also issuing the whistle cry.

"Damn things," Portman said, wiping his boot on the wet grass in an attempt to get the slime the parasite had secreted off.

Dagger looked concerned. "That the venom?" he asked.

Portman shook his head. "Don't think so. Or it would've gone through my boot already," he said.

"Good point," Dagger said, lighting up another cigarette.

The men walked over to the dead worm. Boggs took out his LifeForm, and began snapping photos. He filmed the wounds, the tubular segments, and the worm's bizarre head and mouth area.When he had his fill of worm guts and stench, he addressed the images to Danni on the CAV, and then addressed Dr. Tara and the incoming CAV. The biologists had a higher level of command at CPB. And he wanted them prepared, and safe. It was Recon Elite's job to sniff things out, fire shots, and eliminate if necessary. But the biologists were God.

10.

Before moving on, the men made sure none of the worm's venom was on their clothing. No one wanted another Emoth situation. Boggs thought about Emoth's death, how painfully slow and agonizing it was, how quickly it had taken for the venom to eat through his shoulder, then his chest cavity, and then enter his heart.

Boggs grimaced, doing his best to keep his disappointment from his men. The truth was, despite the drone reconnaissance and data gathering, they'd come unprepared, and two good men had paid the price. Boggs would not make the same mistake again.

From his pack, he deployed a tiny foldable drone the size of a ruler. As he unfolded, a prop on each arm whirred to life, and a red light blinked at the plastic head. Boggs held the drone in one hand, then fired up his LifeForm and scanned a code on the drone's lower section. The devices each beeped once, and the drone was locked to the LifeForm. Boggs gave it a good toss, and the drone hovered above him at twelve feet.

"West," Boggs said into the LifeForm.

The drone flew away, the red light blinking on its nose cone.

Dagger watched as it flew, his eyes half-squinting in the two suns.

"Those things always trip me out," he said. "Still aint gotten used to them yet."

"Well," Boggs said, "they're a man's best friend."

Portman shook his head. "A golden retriever is man's best friend," he said. "Not a fucking piece of plastic."

"Easy," Boggs said. "This piece of plastic is looking out for us."

As the drone headed west and scanned the terrain, Boggs took a sip from his nutrient straw. He had to keep reminding himself to do this, or he'd find his ass in a Life Chamber receiving rehydration sprays. And after watching Emoth suffer in one of those things, that was the *last* place he wanted to be, even though he knew how much good they could do.

Boggs sucked more of the nutrients, relishing the sugary taste. The other men took note of their captain. Dagger even set aside his cigarette for a minute to properly hydrate and sustain himself.

"We need more of this," Boggs said. "We're getting carried away in all the drama. We need to get back to basics, focus on the nuts and bolts that will help keep us alive."

Boggs turned and shaded his eyes. "The drone is scanning for more worms and parasites," he said. "It can reach up to ten feet below ground, detecting any disturbances."

Dagger frowned. "Ten feet isn't shit," he said.

Portman slapped Dagger on the back. "They can also see ahead of us," he said. "And in this tundra environment, they won't get snagged on trees or vegetation. It's a huge help," Portman said. "Give it some time."

Dagger looked around, and held his hands in the air while his cigarette dangled in his mouth. "Time is all we got, boys!" he said. "Take a look around."

He has a point, Boggs thought.

Boggs paused, and let darkness creep into his mind. False images of Sarah and Connor flashed in and out, Connor running through a city lot back on Earth, the polluted air grey and tumultuous behind him as he ran, but his eyes a fierce cobalt, as fierce as Boggs had ever seen. Sarah, post-birth in a red dress, her hair blowing in the wind, skyscrapers and project housing rising to the sky in unending columns. Boggs reached out to her in his mind, mesmerized by her red lipstick. She opened her mouth to call to him, but when she spoke, he heard Staunch's voice instead.

"Sir," Staunch said. "Your LifeForm is beeping."

Boggs looked down. Sure enough, the drone was relaying information back to his device. And it flashed the warning symbol.

"What is it?" Dagger asked.

"Hard to say," Boggs said.

"Better yet, how big is it?" Staunch asked.

Boggs cupped his hands over his eyes to view the screen. "About the size of a wolf, maybe," he said. "Or a pony. Three hundred yards west."

Boggs shouldered his rifle, looked over the dead worm to make sure it wouldn't pop up at the last minute, and headed west.

The men followed.

Every fifty yards, Boggs looked behind his team to make sure the parasites weren't following. They weren't, luckily. But he had a nasty hunch the little devils were just out of sight, monitoring what they were doing.

He had no doubt about that at all.

Boggs and his men sloshed through the bog tundra, kicking up ice water, grass, and soil. Boggs wasn't surprised to see the grass similar to Earth's grass. Sometimes, grass was just fucking grass.

The two suns cast dim light behind the impenetrable clouds as the hike wore on. And for a moment, Boggs wondered if the thing they'd been pursuing had suddenly turned around, and was pursuing *them*.

In a few minutes, the distance was cut in half, and Boggs thought he saw an outline of an animal on the horizon.

There was no sign of the drone, which was weird.

The creature was now close enough that the LifeForm could handle things on its own.

And oddly, the creature was now two hundred yards away, rather than the one hundred and fifty it had just been.

"Damn," Dagger said, clicking in with his own LifeForm. "That thing is chucking," he said.

"Must've seen us," Staunch said.

Boggs felt an odd sensation, and whipped around. Before it disappeared, he caught the eye of a parasite peering over a lump of grass fifty yards behind them.

So they were being followed. Awesome.

Another sensation hit Boggs, except this time it was his COMMS device vibrating in his vest pocket in silent mode.

Boggs made sure no more parasites were coming, then put the device to his jaw.

"Captain, I'm receiving an inbound message from CAV-121,"

Danni said. "Shall I patch them through?"

"Yes of course," Boggs said as his men stopped and watched him, with the exception of Staunch, who had his eyes on the parasites that were now scurrying for a low ridge to the east.

A voice chimed in. A voice Boggs was all too familiar with.

"Sam," the woman's voice said. "Can you hear me?"

"Loud and clear," Boggs said, holding back the emotion in his voice. God damn it was so good to hear her voice.

"It's Dr. Tara," she said. "We're on Mawholla."

"Great news," Boggs said, a genuine smile creeping across his face despite the ominous set of circumstances that surrounded him. He was still alive. And there was nothing wrong in enjoying that fact.

"It's not all great news," Dr. Tara said. "We've had some mechanical issues, and had to land two hundred and eighty miles from the coordinates you'd sent."

Boggs frowned, and shook it off quickly while scanning the horizon for the strange, evasive creature. "We'll come get you," he said. "How many on board?"

"Four," Dr. Tara said. "And a plethora of high-end equipment."

"Do you have weapons?" Boggs asked.

"Of course. We would not come to Mawholla without them, but I'm not entirely thrilled."

Boggs shook his head. "You'll be thrilled as soon as one of those rifles saves your life."

Dr. Tara sighed. "There's no hurry. We're establishing a safety perimeter made of laser fencing, and then proceeding to run base-level experiments. We have enough food and hydration for months."

"Understood," Boggs said. "But we'll be there sooner rather than later."

"Thanks," Dr. Tara said. "And Sam...it's great to hear your voice again."

Before Boggs could respond, the COMM device clicked. She'd hung up.

Dagger shook his head and took a drag off his cigarette. "That woman is all business, eh?"

"Almost always," Boggs said. "And now, she's your boss."

Dagger smirked. "And yours too, sir."

The men exchanged nervous chuckles. Boggs pocketed his COMM device and headed in the direction towards the creature.

"Come on," he said. "We need to finally meet our little friend."

11.

Far off on the horizon, as the fading light of two suns ushered in dusk, Boggs saw a form head up a low ridge.

"Are those trees?" Dagger asked as he used his rifle scope to scan the horizon.

"Yes," Boggs said. "The first ones in forever. They remind me of evergreens back on Earth."

Staunch nodded. "They do indeed."

The wolf-sized animal moved with precision, but not exactly fast as it disappeared into a stand of trees.

"Let's go," Boggs said. "Cloud Four Formation once we hit that ridge. Got it?"

"Yes sir," Portman said, stealing one of Dagger's cigarettes and blocking the flame with his hand.

A half hour later the men reached the base of the low ridge. It was one of those truly otherworldly moments for Boggs, as he took in the gentle rise of the ridge, dotted with pleasant evergreen-looking trees, and two suns dipping in the sky in a film of amber and dusky clouds.

Staunch veered off to the left forty yards, while Dagger and Portman veered right. Boggs would take center and forward positions as he always did. Normally, Emoth would be with him.

Boggs grimaced, and tried to shake it off. There was no time to mourn when you were dealing with the unknown. Once they'd cracked this planet's code, he could drown in all the woe-is-me moments he could muster. And he had a feeling there would be plenty of those to come as long as he could do his job.

But was this really just a job? It was more than that...more like a Hail Mary pass for the human race. Although he received a paycheck, the stakes were the highest of any profession the human race had ever seen. This was a mission to save himself, and all the potential future families. As simple as that.

What good was a paycheck with no home?

As Staunch, Portman, and Boggs cast a net around the unknown creature, the suns dipped behind the ridge, casting a surreal light over this empty portion of Mawholla.

And then the thing they'd been stalking, turned the tables.

It emerged from a clump of trees, the surreal dusk light behind it. Boggs couldn't believe what he was seeing. He wondered if it was a cross between a small cow, a chimpanzee, and a wolf. At least it had the face of a wolf, but the ears of a chimpanzee and the aqua-marine eyes of an American lynx, the rest of its body stocky like a pony, but covered in hair, except for its paws.

There was no doubt in Boggs' mind the thing was intelligent. And when he made eye contact for the first time, a very unpleasant sensation crept up his spine:

Maybe it was more intelligent than they were.

The creature moved forward, and Boggs was surprised to see it stand on hind legs, and use its front legs like a human would use arms.

Staunch, Portman, and Dagger closed the net, and aimed their rifles at the thing.

Boggs held up his hand, and the men eased back, but just a little.

"What the hell is this thing?" Dagger asked, looking none too pleased.

The creature let out a grunt, sort of like a human burp, and watched the men intently with eyes the color of the Florida Keys.

Then, amazingly, the creature beckoned to Boggs with one of its legs.

Boggs shook his head. As the men guarded him, he took out his LifeForm reader to reaffirm the creature's status.

The meter indicated it was dangerous, but Boggs wondered what exactly was triggering that specific status alert. The animal didn't appear dangerous to his eyes, or his instincts. *Yet.*

Boggs studied the creature as it stared back at him with its head cocked, a slight breeze rustling its silver and black fur.

Hmmm, Boggs thought. Maybe it could run fast? Perhaps it could spit that crap like all the other creatures they'd encountered here so far? Or maybe it had lots of friends...the kind that might come out and ambush them at any second.

Dagger spat, and aimed his ZR-15. "I don't like it," he said. "It's giving me a bad feeling."

Portman nodded, as Staunch gripped his rifle harder.

"Permission to kill, sir?" Staunch asked.

Boggs made firm eye contact with the animal once more. The eyes were intelligent...too intelligent. And did Boggs see a smirk?

The thing opened its wolf-like snout, and Boggs aimed his rifle. The thing let out a piercing banshee wail that echoed across Mawholla's skies, and then it simply disappeared. Boggs froze for half a second, and then aimed his rifle around furiously.

"Behind you!" Dagger shouted.

Inexplicably, the creature appeared behind Boggs, and cocked its head, as if taunting him.

Boggs realized he couldn't chance another spitting type-animal, so he made the decision to kill.

He simply dropped his index finger at his side, and his men opened fire.

When the shots had ended and the smoke cleared, the creature was gone.

"3 o'clock," Staunch shouted.

Boggs spun to his right, and the creature appeared once more, opened its wolf-like mouth and snapped its jaws shut, as if teasing the men.

Boggs gave the order again, and his men fired at the creature, which disappeared in the chaos, and then managed to appear once more, this time at 9 o'clock, next to a clump of trees.

Boggs did not give the order this time.

Instead he stared down the creature, admiring either its sheer speed or unheard-of cloaking abilities. The exact cause of its magnificent abilities not yet fully determined. And maybe never if he didn't get his shit together.

Boggs knew one thing for sure: Dr. Tara would have his nuts on a wall if he killed a species that displayed such remarkable abilities.

Boggs wondered. Maybe it was time to try talking to it. He'd been a goon, a meathead, and had pulled the trigger too soon.

"Hey," Boggs said to it as the thing cocked its head at him. "What are you, and how in the heck are you able to pull off that neat trick?"

The creature cocked its head once more, and emitted a series of bark like cries, mixed in with more language-like vocalizations.

"It's trying to talk," Dagger said. "Holy shit."

"You got that right," Staunch said. "Fuckin' crazy."

Boggs briefly checked his periphery to make sure the parasites weren't stalking them again, and turned his attention back to the creature, which continued to stare at them as if they were mice to a big tomcat.

"Hey," Boggs said. "I'm sorry about that whole shoot-em-up earlier. We pulled the trigger too soon. We're an excitable bunch."

Boggs pointed to his chest. "My name is Sam," he said. "Sam Boggs." Then Boggs pointed back at the creature. "Do you have a n-a-m-e?"

The creature cocked its head, opened its wolf jaws and emitted another series of barks and language-like vocalizations.

Then it turned and ran up the slope, kicking bits of tundra grass and soil as it ran.

Dagger looked confused. "You're just going to let it go?"

"Yes," Boggs said. "I fucked up by firing on it, got paranoid about the spitter type of animals," he said. "This is not a spitter variation. This is something very special."

Portman shook his head, and slapped Staunch on the shoulder.

"You hear that," Portman said. "The captain just admitted he was wrong."

All three men chuckled.

"That's a first," Staunch said.

"Alright, alright," Boggs said. "We've had enough fun at my expense for now. Let's let this thing regroup with the rest of its kind, and get back to the CAV so we can meet up with Dr. Tara. They're going to want a full report on this speedy species, the worm, the reptile spitters, and the parasites. It's been a hell of a long day. Good work, men."

12.

Once the men were settled into the CAV-117, Boggs turned on what was left of the shield, and sat in a chair near the monitor consoles. He switched from view to view, occasionally flashing back to the big momma spitters that had tormented the ship last night.

God there'd been so many, he thought.

It made Boggs not want to venture into the forested areas in the future. He pondered schemes, wondered if he and his men could somehow skirt around that issue. Maybe the CPB would declare the forested zone "off limits", and make the rest of Mawholla a settlement zone.

But deep down he knew that was bullshit.

The biologists would have answers for the spitters, and hopefully for the wolf-like creature that could evade the brute force of a Recon Elite team, as if they were mere jokes. And he had to admit, the latter half of the day he'd felt like a punchline. He'd panicked with the wolf-thing, and pulled the trigger too soon. On a planet where Boggs knew only a few people, there'd be a time where he needed to make allies with the animals they discovered here. One thing was certain, the drones and unmanned research craft had all been wrong. There was more life here than originally documented.

Boggs grinned, in an unnerving sort of way.

It was no damn wonder the wolf-thing had never been picked up by the first drones and research craft.

It simply vanished.

Then why had it let the foldable drone track it today? Boggs wondered.

And the answer to that was all too clear.

It *wanted* the men to track it. Because once again, it enjoyed toying with them.

Boggs took a deep breath, and tried to wrap his head around Mawholla.

The overwhelming psychological aspects of planetary exploration was vastly underrated and under-taught in military school. The emphasis was on order, cleanliness, orientation and dissemination of effective violence. The briefings by CPB were light on psychology as well, with more emphasis on "for the greater good" jargon.

Not once, not even once, was the psychology of being one of only a few men on a new planet covered.

He fought it back, the massive, crushing silence of a wilderness planet brimming with bizarre creatures. It weighed on him in ways few other men had ever experienced. Humans were new at this after all. He was the spearhead.

A prominent engineer on Earth had created a physics breakthrough in space travel, mostly involving propulsion. Another engineer had devised the "Happy Boxes." In a matter of several years, these breakthroughs had aligned, and the first CAV's fit for long-term human travel had been designed.

An enormous chunk of money and manpower had gone into their production. After all, what good was money on a dying planet?

And that was the funny thing. The entire human race facing death once the U.N. scientists declared another hundred years on Earth, max, the societal fabric had begun to tear at the seams. Things just seemed to matter less and less.

Well, except for one thing.

The ships.

And of course, the men and resources required to launch them.

And what kind of men would best be suited?

Already trained men (mostly). And fit men, like soldiers. Men who could execute an order while maintaining a semblance of cohesion. Men like Sam Boggs, Tim Emoth, and James T Bone. Men who were already stationed in places like Libya, making sure the Middle East didn't disintegrate, and take the rest of the world with it prematurely.

They'd always been good soldiers, and now they'd be transformed from taking out terrorists, to becoming Lewis and Clark with way, way better weapons.

Boggs sighed, and thumbed a photo of Sarah that he kept in his right pant pocket. She was so beautiful. A wall of melancholy built up in him and almost welled to tears before fading.

Big boys don't cry, Boggs thought.

A moment later, Danni chimed in. "Captain, you have a call," she said.

"Accept," Boggs said.

A voice came through the console speakers as his men slept in bunks within section 2 of the CAV.

"Sam," Dr. Tara said. "We're surrounded by really impressive life forms. But they're giving us a really hard time," she said. "You're needed."

"On it," Boggs said.

"Thank you," Dr. Tara said.

Boggs stood, and flipped on the engines. "Danni, get us to Dr. Tara's coordinates as quickly as possible, within safety guidelines."

"Yes Captain," Danni said.

Boggs slammed a cup of coffee, and went back to his men. There would not be much sleep tonight.

13.

When the CAV-117 hovered above the biologist's CAV, Boggs saw exactly what he was expecting: several big momma spitters chewing on the CAV-121, sending up blue streaks of electricity that spidered across the ship, but also down the length of the big mommas and into the ground.

"Fuckin' things," Staunch said as he tore into microwavable meatloaf.

The sight of the big mommas tearing at Dr. Tara's ship almost made Boggs panic for a moment.

Almost.

But he knew the woman was actually tougher than he was. Much tougher.

As Danni set the CAV down forty yards from the biologist's CAV, Boggs studied the forested environment.

The same principle seemed to apply. The spitters were an edge species, meaning that's where they preferred to hunt. They'd stalk prey from the tree line, then pounce and corral them in open meadows. So why exactly did employees and military under the command of CPB keep landing in ten acre meadows at the edge of tree line?

That was a damn good question.

Boggs hit his COMM button on the console.

"Can you fly that thing out of there?" he asked Dr. Tara. "They like forest openings."

"Not yet," Dr. Tara said. "There's too many on the ship."

"Okay," Boggs said.

He shouldered a ZR-15, then slapped the ramp button and descended into the humid Mawholla night. His men followed him. As soon as Recon Elite Six squared up with the big mommas and a few smaller spitters, Boggs gave the order to open fire.

Gunfire shattered the wilderness silence. The big mommas roared and turned to face Recon Elite.

"Again," Boggs said.

The men fired, cutting down a smaller spitter and sending a piece of its jagged skull slapping against a big momma's leg.

"Jesus," Dagger shouted. "There's so damn many. We need more firepower."

Boggs hurried up the ramp into the CAV, and grabbed the canon joystick. The external guns whirred to life, sending round after round into the spitters, big and small. As Boggs watched the monitors, the scent of metal burning and gunpowder filled his nostrils. He wondered what in the hell it was like out there.

The spitters could only take so much fire.

The smaller ones staggered around, missing legs and tails and whatever the hell else they grew out of their weird bodies. The big mommas had seen and felt enough, gaping holes in soft underbellies gushing blood and in some cases their bulbous entrails. They turned and headed for the cover of trees, not roaring, not screeching, but quietly, like a dog that had been whipped by an asshole for an owner.

Boggs heard Dagger whooping it up from below, and soon joined his men. But not before flipping on his LifeForm meter, just to make sure none of the spitters came back.

But it wasn't enough.

Boggs spoke into his COMM device on Dr. Tara's frequency. "You holding up okay?" he asked.

"Thank you," she said breathlessly. "We didn't have time to get our Nubar Fence deployed."

"What the hell is a Nubar Fence?" Boggs asked.

"Watch," Dr. Tara said.

A moment later a cylinder the size of a man ejected from the top hatch on the biologists' CAV.

The cylinder rolled into the center of the meadow, and then a laser net emitted from a camera-like lens on its exterior. Bright, pulsing green shone in a 360 degree radius, covering the men and the ships in green glow before stopping at the tree line. The cylinder cracked in half, and eight mini-drones rolled into every point on the compass towards the trees. A shrill beep emitted from the cylinder, and before Boggs could blink, a crisscrossed laser fence thirty feet high completely encased the two CAVs and his men, along with the precise outline of the meadow.

Dagger stood there, mouth slack.

"Well I'll be," he said. "Never seen anything like it."

"That makes four of us," Boggs said. "But I'm not surprised. The biologists always have a bag of tricks."

Boggs heard the biologists' CAV ramp lower, and he felt dry sensation in his throat.

In the backlight of CAV-121, Dr. Tara strolled down the ramp, dressed in camouflage waterproof jacket, a plastic toolbox in her right hand. Behind her, two men and a woman followed, the green glow of the crisscrossed laser fence making them all seem almost alien.

Boggs and his team met the new arrivals halfway between each ship.

Dr. Tara hugged Boggs, and he felt himself melting, then recovered as quickly as possible.

Boggs couldn't help but be smitten with her. Everything about her, from her long hair to her mannerisms drew him in. But he told himself to be professional, to act like a fucking man. And so he did.

Dr. Tara turned to her team.

"Recon Six," she said, pointing to a tall skinny man. "This is Dr. Reynolds." Dr. Tara gestured to the Asian woman, who wore a pair of spectacles. "This is Dr. Mana," she said. "And last but not least, is Dr. Volter."

The groups exchanged handshakes, and Boggs found himself pleased to be socializing, however briefly with other human beings. No, not just pleased, RELIEVED. For the briefest of moments, he felt the sheer vast expanse of this wilderness planet pull back and let his nerves relax.

Dr. Tara looked around the meadow, a smug grin on her face. "How do you like our new fencing system?" she asked Boggs.

"What's not to like," he said.

"Right," she said. "Not much impresses you. You've seen it all."

Boggs was a bit taken aback by her snark, then recovered. "Ma'am," he said, "A day on Mawholla *is* seeing it all."

Dr. Tara frowned.

All around them, thousands of night insects buzzed and chirped, not all that different from what they had in rainforest ecosystems back on Earth.

And that was the thing.

Star Trek was bullshit.

Most of the planets were desert wastelands, with whatever life forms left whittled down to reptilian slithering things. Or the ice planets, which mostly contained dangerous bacteria.

The animals were slight variations of what had been on Earth, and what was on Earth right now. There wasn't some magic ball that shot out super insane eighteen dimensional gaseous monsters. Humans, animals on Earth, and animals on other planets were all the same fucking stardust, random variations on a theme.

The spitters were a lot like dinosaurs, especially the Dilophosaurus before they went extinct.

The biggest differences were the planets themselves.

Boggs eyed the dark forest beyond the laser fencing, and thought he saw a pair of big momma eyes glittering back there. Maybe one of them nursing its wounds. Maybe one of them dying.

Boggs had a few simple rules. He was actually, and had always been an animal person. Ever since he was a kid fishing for perch and bass in his Uncle Jedy's pond. He loved petting zoos, loved learning about animals, could not read enough about them.

But he did have rules.

Spiders needed to not touch him. They could go on their own way otherwise. The same rule applied to the spitters, or any other thing they'd come across.

Give us space.

Don't attack.

If a new animal species complied with these two rules, there was never a reason to shoot any of them. Why would they? The goal was to *inhabit* a planet, not kill everything and ruin it like they did to Earth, their mother.

"Place is starting to feel like home," Staunch said from behind Boggs. "As fucked up as it's been."

Boggs took a deep breath.

Maybe it was. Maybe.

14.

Luckily, the biologists' CAV had not experienced the exterior damage that CAV-117 had. And the quirky engine issues and other problems the crew had first experienced had been solved by Portman and Dr. Volter.

What hadn't been solved was the exterior damage to the CAV-117. The craft still wouldn't be able to leave orbit, and Boggs wondered if it ever would, even if it could be repaired.

Dr. Volter was built like a stocky wrestler, not tall, but not wimpy either. A scar ran down his neck, as if something had bitten or clawed him a long time ago. Boggs tried not to stare, but he didn't have to try to not ask questions. He minded his own business.

For the most part.

Dr. Volter dropped the wrench he'd been using on the CAV-117's roof. "It's damaged at 80%" levels," he said.

Dagger shouted from below. "How would you know?" he asked.

"Because I designed the CAV series," Dr. Volter said.

Boggs chuckled. The biologists were always full of surprises.

"So biology and engineering?" Boggs asked.

Dr. Volter nodded as he thumbed a tablet. "We learn to multitask at the academy these days. We're like sharks. You have to swim to stay alive."

"I get it," Boggs said. "They are amazing spacecraft. I'm impressed, Dr."

"What's impressive," Dr. Volter said, "is you six coming here, losing two of your men, and still managing to hold your ground. That takes great courage and skill."

"It's just our job," Boggs said.

"So is this," Dr. Volter said as he walked across the top of the CAV-117, and kneeled about twenty feet from the engine exhaust ports.

He took out a medallion-looking device, and laid it flat into a hollow receptacle. Boggs heard a *click*, and a seven by seven foot chunk of the ship's hull slid back, revealing a neatly-stacked column of spare heat–reflecting tiles-exactly what the big mommas had ripped off.

Boggs sighed. "I need to read the manual next time."

"It's not a worry," Dr. Volter said. "I always design redundancies. I would have informed you had you informed me."

Boggs felt guilty. "Next time, I'll let you know right away," he said.

The men worked on replacing the missing and damaged heat shields as the laser fence hummed and buzzed. Every so often, fat, moth-like insects flew into the fence, frying into little bits and pieces. Sometimes Boggs caught the scent of cooking flesh, and glimpsed bits of wings falling to Mawholla on fire.

A moment later, Dr. Tara climbed the ladder and stepped over to the men.

"In the morning," she said, "we need to run tests on what you call 'spitters'."

Dr. Tara tapped Boggs on the shoulder, as he kneeled and helped with the repairs.

"Sam," Dr. Tara said. "Look."

Boggs followed her pointing finger, waiting for his eyes to adjust to the darkness behind the laser fence. When they finally did, a pair of big momma eyes stared back, soon joined by another.

"They've been a huge problem," Boggs said. "And I'm not betting on that fence holding them forever. They're smart, real smart."

Dr. Tara frowned. "We ran some LifeForm tests on the way down, that were much more powerful than the drones we sent initially to Mawholla," she said. "They indicated a larger, dangerous species. The other interesting thing, is that we found vast layers of honeycomb tunnels or burrows beneath the forested sections of Mawholla. Now, the 'spitters' as you call them don't appear to be designed for living, or even part-time living underground. They are certainly forest creatures, or mountain creatures designed for surface ambush." Dr. Tara regarded the group with curiosity. "Did any of you see cave entrances, or anything that could be taken as a burrow entrance?"

Boggs shook his head. "Not that I know of. But we did come across an enormous worm in the northern tundra. It's possible that thing's species could be responsible for all the tunnels."

"It's possible," Dr. Tara said as she inspected a portion of a loose heat shield in her hand. "Can you send me images of the worm?"

"I can do better than that," Boggs said. "I can take you there tomorrow."

15.

Boggs, Dr. Tara, Dr. Mana, and Staunch made the journey in the freshly repaired CAV-117. The biologists had decided that the meadow where they'd set up the laser fence would be Base Camp 1. From there, they'd explore what they could of Mawholla before making any final determinations.

Danni landed the CAV-117 fifty yards from where the worm carcass had laid the night before. But when the group approached the battle scene, most of the worm had been picked apart by scavengers.

Boggs looked for the parasites, but none could be found. Instead, a large bird soared overhead, reminding Boggs of a California condor, which had gone extinct hundreds of years ago.

Another bird soon followed, and it was clear to Boggs the birds were at least partly responsible for contributing to the demise of the worm carcass.

Boggs kicked a hunk of the worm with his boot, exposing a clump of wriggling maggot-like creatures.

Dr. Tara and Dr. Mana moved in with their equipment.

"Hold up," Boggs said. "This is one of the spitting variety. I told you about what happened to Emoth and T-Bone. The stuff will melt right through your skin, then travel up your arteries and seize your heart if you get enough of it on you."

"Noted," Dr. Mana said. Then she pulled out a small recording device. "Recon Six spearhead indicates worm species is venomous, similar to reptile-like species. Extreme caution must be used in all sample collections."

Dr. Tara frowned as she poked a pointer into one of the worm's half-eaten tubular sections.

Then she shook her head, running the pointer along a rough contour of worm meat, about two by two feet wide.

"See this?" she said.

"Yeah," Boggs said.

"We had something big in here last night," Dr. Tara said."These are bite marks."

"Great," Boggs said.

He wondered if it was the spitters, or something else entirely.

Dr. Tara and Dr. Mana worked over the eaten worm, measuring bite marks while being careful not to touch anything.

"It's clear the biter is an animal that walks on all fours," she said, "based on bite angle."

"Is it anything we need to take care of?" Boggs asked.

"We don't know yet," Dr. Tara said.

"It's possible this is a herbivore," Dr. Mana said. "Some of these bite marks left molar-like impressions."

Boggs turned and gazed at the western horizon. Did his eyes just play tricks on him, or had something moved out there?

Yes, something had moved, and was moving. A line of them, looking like lions with even more hair, sprinting their way hard and fast, kicking up tundra in a cloud of mud and grass.

"Go," Boggs said, grabbing Dr. Tara by the arm and yanking her towards the CAV. She tried to reach for her toolbox, but Boggs yanked her away.

In the commotion, in the mayhem, this was where Boggs thrived. While the biologists had significant book intelligence, Boggs had physical intelligence. Everything slowed down *except* for him. He heard Staunch shouting as more of the lion-like creatures appeared on a low ridge to the east of the worm carcass. They too, charged at full speed.

Boggs shoved Dr. Tara towards the CAV, then raised his ZR-15, set it to *decimate*, and fired into the closest pack of creatures from the east. Most of the creatures thundered on, but he'd injured two of them. As the new species gained on them, Boggs was horrified by their oddly long jaws and rows of teeth. The new species had the eyes of the primate species Aye-Aye, and the hair of lions, but the underbelly and jaws were those of a crocodile. Boggs had never in his life seen anything like it. So he gave them a name. *Lerkas.*

"Get your fucking asses to the CAV," he ordered Dr. Tara and Dr. Mana in-between bursts of rifle fire.

Staunch chucked a frag grenade and timed it perfectly, obliterating three creatures as the others roared in terror at what had happened to their comrades.

But still the lerkas kept coming.

The creatures closed in from the east and west, and then dispersed, forming a pincer movement that would no doubt turn Boggs and his people into an easy meal.

But Boggs was having none of it. He chucked a frag nade at the western pack of creatures, exploding the head of the lead animal.

"Fuck this," Staunch said. "They're outnumbering us."

Boggs concurred. "Back to the CAV," he said. "Pronto."

Boggs and Staunch hustled back to the ship and easily caught up with Dr. Mana. She was too slow, so Boggs reduced his speed to protect her.

"Come on," he shouted. "You gotta be faster!"

Dr. Mana said nothing, only stared at the ship with bulging eyes as she pumped her arms.

But it wasn't enough.

Boggs dropped to one knee and raised his ZR-15, firing off several rounds and chucking a frag nade to the east. He quickly pivoted and engaged the western pack with as much firepower as he and Staunch could muster.

Boggs could see the creatures' eyes now, big and amber, with pupils like slits. Their tongues stuck out the sides of their narrow mouths. But they did not snap their jaws, that would expend too much energy. Instead the creatures' jaws remained shut in a creepy, frozen state as they ogled their next meal.

Boggs fired off thirty rounds as numerous creatures died and howled around him. Staunch cried out in pain as he was bit in the arm. The smell of shit and guts and brains filled a cloud of grass and ice water. In the commotion Boggs heard Dr. Mana cry out. One of the creatures had taken her and dragged her away, and as the western and eastern packs converged, they pounced on her and separated her limbs from her torso as blood sprayed in wild arcs.

Staunch let loose a frag grenade into the hungry pack, blowing the legs off a creature and instantly killing Dr. Mana.

Boggs and Staunch retreated up the CAV ramp, as Dr. Tara punched the button on the wall to seal it.

"Where is Dr. Mana?" she asked, her wide eyes pleading for a positive answer.

Boggs just shook his head. "She didn't make it," he said.

Dr. Tara put her hand to her mouth and paced around the ship's cabin.

"What do you mean she didn't make it?" Dr. Tara asked. "She was a respected colleague, one of the best."

"The new species got her," Boggs said. "We tried our best. She couldn't keep up. We did everything we could to protect her."

Staunch flipped on the external cameras, and the three of them watched as the creatures howled and fought with each other near the worm carcass. One of them was dragging a spine and bones.

"Turn it off," Dr. Tara said.

Boggs turned off the monitor.

"Danni," he said. "Return us to Base Camp 1."

The CAV-117 fired up, and soon the three of them were flying over the uninhabited maw of Mawholla, wondering what the hell was going to happen next.

It was always something.

15.

What was left of Recon Elite and the biologists held a small service for Dr. Mana, T-Bone, and Emoth. The CAVs were equipped with eternal projectors, and these were programmed to flash images accrued from the deceased's social media pages and official online accounts.

Boggs did not tear up.

Oh, he wanted to, but he wouldn't let himself. Dr. Tara was beside herself, and Boggs wondered if she had been as poorly equipped to deal with the psychological ramification of planetary colonization as everyone else. She'd lost not only a respected peer, but a friend as well.

Boggs led Dr. Tara outside, protected by the humming glow of the laser fences. When he was certain he was out of view of his men, he held his arms out wide.

Dr. Tara smiled through her tears, and embraced him.

"This is such fuckery," she said. "All of it. We'd been prepped Sam by the CPB. Days of it prior to launch."

"Days?" Boggs said. "This kind of thing needs weeks, even years."

Dr. Tara shook her head. "They saved the best for engineering the spacecraft," she said. "We were the rushed part."

"I get it," Boggs said. "I really do. I wish there was something I could do. It sucks losing people. We've never lost team members so fast."

"It did happen fast," Dr. Tara said. "Brutally fast. One second we're collecting samples, and the next I'm seeing my colleague's spine dragged across the tundra by wild animals."Dr. Tara cried, and gripped Boggs' shirt with both fists.

He remained quiet and kept his words to himself as she let it all out into his shoulder. That was all he could do.

"And the worst part Sam, is she had two kids back home, Aaron and Ashley. Just five and three years old."

Boggs shook his head. "I'm sorry for your loss."

Dr. Tara let up on her sobbing, then let go of Boggs and headed towards the glowing laser fence. Above her, a moth-looking insect fluttered into the lasers, let out a shriek, and burst into flames.

Dr. Tara cried again. "This," she said, pointing at the fence. "This is what we do, Sam. It's all so clear now, isn't it? We find a perfectly good planet, existing, no…co-existing, and we come along and mess it up. We erect our technology without a thought except for ourselves."

Dr. Tara gestured to the glowing fence.

"Perfect example," she said. "We erected this for us. But we did it without even considering what it would to any life forms other than us. That's the human way. And I fear, I really do, that we won't learn on Mawholla, either."

Boggs stepped toward her, his hands glowing green from the fence. "Something in the forest might've eaten that moth," he said. "And we didn't know how long it would live anyway. Moths have short lifespans."

"I know," Dr. Tara said. "You're talking to a biologist, you goof. I'm letting my emotions get the best of me. I'm sorry," she said. "This isn't professional at all."

Dr. Tara made watery eye contact with him. "Captain Boggs," she said, "order me to get my shit together."

Boggs chuckled. "I'm not going to do that."

"Do it," Dr. Tara ordered.

Boggs held his tongue. He checked beyond the laser fence, thinking he saw movement back there, but couldn't be sure.

"You did what you could," Boggs said.

"That's the thing," Dr. Tara said. "I didn't. I ran away. Ran past her, left her to die."

Overhead, a shooting star arced an opening in the clouds, then simmered into the black.

Bizarre bird calls emanated from the forest all around them. At least the birds seemed to avoid the fence, as far as what Boggs had seen. But he had to wonder about Dr. Tara's points.

It *did* feel weird, like they were repeating history. Already, they'd had an impact. But it didn't feel like the missions on the other planets. Those places were fucked. The fence, and even the CAVs felt like warts, or a virus upon Mawholla. And when they finally got the Ark-01 large scale transport ships completed on Earth, there'd be much, much more of it.

Boggs looked at the stars, and the half-assed laser fence, and their CAVs.

Junk, he thought. And the very reason why humans got into the mess they were in. Too much crap. Too much attachment to the material.

When compared to the creatures that killed Dr. Mana today, or even that weird wolf-looking animal yesterday, humans were inherently weaker. They needed a hell of a lot of crap to function.

"I know what you're thinking," Dr. Tara said. "You're thinking like I was, Sam. I'm trying to fight it. I keep trying the cheerleader technique, you know? Rha-Rha-Rha, go Team Humans! Yay!...but it's not working."

Boggs took Dr. Tara's hand. "I felt the same way," he said. "When we lost T-Bone and Emoth. And I do feel guilty about mucking up a pristine planet. But there's something else in me, too. Something stronger than the doubts."

"And what is that, Sam?" Dr. Tara asked.

"Survival," Boggs said. "It supersedes everything."

Dr. Tara nodded, and glanced up at the stars, craning her neck. "We ruined our mother," she said. "We ruined the very place that gave birth to our species."

Boggs stared up at the millions of stars and frowned. "We did," he said. "But we didn't destroy Earth. She'll come around in a hundred thousand years. What we did, was we destroyed mother earth for *us*. She'll still be there, spinning."

"The CPB is going to implement extremely harsh environmental laws here," Dr. Tara said. "So we don't repeat."

"It's going to be necessary," Boggs said.

"And the monetary system. It's going away eventually," she said. "They're implementing A Shared-Economy-System in twenty years."

Boggs was shocked by that one. "They're taking away money?"

"Eventually," Dr. Tara said. "That's the very definition of harsh environmental laws. Money breeds corruption, and corruption hits land management and chemical regulation the hardest. Always has."

Boggs tightened his fingers into a fist. He didn't like the idea of his paychecks going away, but Dr. Tara had a point. Money was the ultimate influencer...good and bad.

Dr. Tara procured a flask of whiskey from her jacket pocket, and took a good, hard swig.

"Damn," Boggs said. "Where did you get that?"

Dr. Tara looked at him lovingly. "Does it matter?"

"Suppose not," Boggs said.

Dr. Tara handed Boggs the flask, and he relished the strong fluid stinging his throat.

"Feeling better?" Dr. Tara said as she smirked at him.

"Sure," he said. "And you are too. I can tell by that grin."

"I'm trying," she said.

Boggs put his arm around her shoulder. "That makes two of us," he said.

16.

In the morning, Boggs and Dagger flew back towards the worm carcass and body-bagged what was left of Dr. Mana. Boggs promised Dr. Tara he'd do this, and he wasn't a man who broke promises.

Despite the bad luck they'd encountered here, Boggs preferred the tundra areas of Mawholla more than the forest country. And he was anxious to encounter the wolf-like creature again, and to learn more about it.

The biologist group had stayed behind at Base Camp 1, running tests beyond the laser perimeter. Staunch and Portman were providing support.

When they'd finished loading Dr. Mana's remains onto the CAV, Boggs and Dagger slipped into backcountry backpacks, and loaded up with frag grenades and a hell of a lot of ZR-15 ammo. The plan was to head to what they'd labeled "Pine Tree Ridge", the place where they'd first encountered the blindingly quick wolf-like creature.

The light was good upon the tundra as the two suns hovered well over the horizon. And surprisingly, it was a cloud free day, which was unusual for Mawholla. The pristine sky rolled on, an endless deep azure.

"What if those lerka things come back?" Dagger said as the men headed for Pine Tree Ridge.

"They won't," Boggs said as he gestured to where the worm had been. "There's nothing left of the carcass. And that's all they were doing, protecting their kill like a bear would. We just happened to be in the wrong place at the wrong time."

The ground was soft under Boggs' boot as they worked towards the ridge, which Boggs could see through his field binoculars.

"Why don't we just fly there?" Dagger asked.

"Those trees might be its habitat, its home," Boggs said. "If we just set the CAV down there, it's clumsy as hell. Dr. Tara agrees. In order to see what exactly is going on here, we need to be a bit more organic in our approach."

"Like organic bananas," Dagger said, gripping his ZR-15.

"Yes, like organic bananas," Boggs said, wincing as he spoke the words.

"Dr. Tara also gave us these," he said, setting down his rifle for a moment and retrieving two thumb drive devices from his pocket. He handed one of the devices to Dagger.

Dagger examined the device, flipping it over in his hand. "What is it?" he asked.

Boggs grinned, and took out an object the size of a lens cap, and tossed it onto the ground near his feet. Then he pressed the red button on the thumb drive device, and aimed it away from his body. As he did, a thin green bendable laser appeared from the device, humming and sizzling. Then Boggs let go of the red button, and drew another laser. Once the two lasers connected, a curved laser fence formed around Boggs, ten feet by ten feet. Boggs felt claustrophobic being encased like this, but he knew he was well-protected.

"Holy shit," Dagger said. "Coolest fucking thing I've ever seen."

Boggs clicked the thumb drive twice, and the lasers disappeared. He tossed Dagger another lens cap device.

"Try it," Boggs said. "You need to practice."

Dagger did as instructed. It took him a few tries, but once the two lasers touched, it signaled the lens cap device to complete the fence structure.

Boggs watched Dagger like a proud father as the glowing laser fence surrounded him.

"Great work," Boggs said, mindful of Dagger's limited training.

Dagger clicked the button a couple times, and the fence disappeared.

"Wicked," Dagger said. "If those lerka things come at us, they're in for a very fun surprise."

"Yes they will be," Boggs said, wondering exactly how many lerkas it would take before the fence failed. Boggs knew there was no way in hell it could ward off dozens of the creatures. Maybe half a dozen.

With the portable safety fences pocketed, Boggs and Dagger continued the hike to Pine Tree Ridge.

Boggs wondered what had ever happened to their drone, on the fateful evening it encountered the wolf-like creature. Had the creature, or its herd caught the drone and dispensed with it? Had the drone simply gone haywire, and now circled the planet on a loop?

Hard to tell.

There was no sign of it anywhere.

Boggs stopped, and scanned the horizon with his binoculars. For a brief moment he caught movement to the south. He recognized the silhouettes.

The lerkas.

Boggs figured the CAV-117 was the attractant. Last night, the CAV had meant fresh food, or soon-to-be fresh food, both in the form of the giant worm, and Dr. Mana (as distasteful as the thought was). The lerkas no doubt saw it flying, and trailed them back to the area of the worm carcass.

"Come on," Boggs said, hurrying Dagger to the north.

"What is it sir?" Dagger asked as he sprinted.

"The lerkas," Boggs said.

"Oh shit," Dagger said. "How many?"

"Enough," Boggs said.

Boggs turned to the southern horizon, and watched as a dozen lerkas sped towards them, clumps of grass and water forming a misty cloud as the creatures thundered.

"Keep going," Boggs said. "We need to reach higher ground."

Before Boggs could say another word, he felt his boots skim through grass.

And that was it.

He found himself tumbling into darkness, smashing his arms and legs against slick rock walls. Dagger screamed below him, as he was the first to enter.

The air in Boggs' lungs expunged painfully as he finally met bottom. His ZR-15 rifle clanked to the hard ground, while Dagger laid there, holding his knee and moaning.

"Fuck," Dagger said. "My knee. What did I do to my fucking knee?"

Boggs shook off the aching pain that wracked his body and put on his headlamp.

Dagger lay there before him, curled in a ball, his eyes wide like that of a prey animal.

Above them, the lerka pack stampeded across the tundra. They probably knew the holes better than anything. But it did give Boggs pause as to why they didn't even investigate. Surely they had a keen sense of smell to locate where he and Dagger had disappeared.

Maybe, just maybe the lerkas knew not to mess with the caves.

Boggs raised Dagger's pant leg to get a better look at his knee. Nothing broken, it seemed, just a good bruise.

"You'll be able to walk this off," Boggs said, ignoring what were for certain his own bruises.

"Okay," Dagger said, clenching his teeth. "Just give me a minute."

Boggs surveyed the cave with his headlamp, lighting up slick, glistening walls. He could see his breath, too, in long cloudy mists. At the far end of the cave, a tunnel maybe three feet wide by three feet tall was partially hidden by a mini-waterfall.

Boggs shined his light into the tunnel, wondering if something was in there waiting. He caught a brief glimpse of something, an animal staring back at him, and quickly realized it was the face of the wolf-like creature. Boggs wondered if his pounding heart was going to burst through his throat.

The creature stared at him with its knowing eyes, then emitted yips and barks mixed with language-like inflections.

And then it was gone.

"What the fuck was that?" Dagger asked as he slowly stood.

"The wolf thing," Boggs said. "It was staring back at me from inside the tunnel."

"Oh, that's not creepy at all," Dagger said.

Bits of dirt and rock tumbled to the cave floor, and Boggs put his finger to his lips.

The lerkas.

They pounded the surface, roaring and caterwauling as they passed the cave entrance.

"Fuck those things," Dagger said.

A shaft of light pierced the entrance, showing Boggs exactly why there was no way out-at least not the way they came in.

Steep, slick walls that not even a monkey could climb surrounded the entrance, which was at least thirty feet above them.

"Nice," Dagger said. "Danni was right, this place is laced with all kinds of this shit."

Boggs watched Dagger limp around the cavern, exhaling his cigarette and panicking as he realized the only way out of this particular cavern was the creepy ass tunnel.

"Fuck that thing," Dagger said.

Boggs took him by the shoulders, with a moderate grip. "You got this," he said.

"I'm claustrophobic," Dagger said. "This place is already getting to me."

"I get it," Boggs said. "I am too. But it's a mind over matter thing. Put it this way. We've got a ton of gear to keep us going, and…ready for the best part?"

"Yeah," Dagger said.

"The best part is we're only thirty feet below the surface of Mawholla. Think about that for a second. That's nothing."

Dagger stared up at the ray of sunlight that punched through the hole. "You're right," he said. "I can still see light."

Boggs patted him on the back. "Good man," he said.

"But you're going fucking first," Dagger said as he punched off the cherry on his cigarette, and pocketed the filter.

Boggs bent over and shined his light into the natural tunnel, then crouched into it, and began to push forward, his hands flush on the walls. Occasionally, his slung ZR-15 rifle scraped against the rocks, making way too much noise.

A moment later, Dagger followed him in.

"You see that thing again?" Dagger whispered.

"No," Boggs said.

"I bet it pops up again," Dagger whispered from behind him. "Right when we least expect it."

"Awesome," Boggs said, not looking forward to that at all.

"It's a crafty fucker," Dagger whispered. "Maybe it's luring us to its lair, so it can eat us."

"Come on," Boggs said.

"Just saying," Dagger said.

Boggs began to feel his mild claustrophobia weigh on him. This sort of thing wasn't uncommon at all, and he especially noticed it amongst taller, bigger men. He'd seen men with much worse cases than his, and that was a nice, strong bearing for pushing forward.

Another fifty yards in, the tunnel veered at a right angle. But instead of taking himself all the way around the bend, Boggs only let his head poke around the corner.

Just in case.

He aimed his headlamp down the new section of tunnel. This one was even longer. And at the end of it, the weird wolf-like thing was staring back at him. It let out several yips, then emitted the vocalizations again.

"I hear it," Dagger said. "That creepy fucking thing!"

"Shhhh," Boggs said.

The creature tilted its head and looked at Boggs with its crazy eyes, and disappeared.

"Shit", Boggs said. "Double shit."

"Fuck," Dagger said. "I can't see what's going on."

"Look behind you," Boggs said, wondering if they were about to be hit from behind.

Dagger grunted as he craned his neck. "Nothing," he said.

"You sure?" Boggs asked.

"I wouldn't say 'nothing' if I wasn't sure there was 'nothing'," Dagger said. "I ain't that green, Captain."

"Good," Boggs said.

He pushed deeper into the tunnel, wondering when that thing would show its face again, and make the odd yipping noise. Boggs also wondered if the creature was actually helping them. Would it, and could it lead the people who'd tried to kill it to safety?

It would take one hell of a patient, yet forgiving life form to do such a thing. But Boggs thought perhaps this creature was exactly that.

Dagger echoed his thoughts, eerily. "I think it's friendly," he said. "Predators, they would've killed us by now, or tried to. Predators don't waste their energy. They need to move, eat, move."

"Interesting points," Boggs said.

"Yep," Dagger said. "I learned a thing or two back in Colorado."

Boggs angled his head back towards Dagger. "You holding up?" he asked.

Dagger sighed. "I'm better than I was at the start of this mission," he said. "I'm sorry about that, sir. They just…they just didn't prepare me for this. I know how to shoot, know how to pack gear, know how to take orders. Know how to push a few buttons on a ship. But there's a whole 'nother side to this they don't explain to you. But I'm figuring it out, slow but steady."

"Good," Boggs said. "I knew you would."

Boggs pushed on ahead into the dark tunnel wondering just what the wolf-like creature had in store for them.

"We need a name for it," Dagger said from behind. "Can't just keep calling it creature, or thing or whatever. We're going to make our home here. The spitters have a name. Now this one is due."

Boggs thought for a moment. "Jekyll," he said. "Because the damn thing can switch speeds like a crazy person can switch personality."

Dagger chuckled. "I like it," he said.

Boggs shined his headlamp deep into the tunnel, but Jekyll had vanished.

After crawling deeper into the tunnel, Boggs heard a scarping sound-a sound Jekyll hadn't made before.

Boggs turned to Dagger awkwardly in the cramped tunnel. "You see anything behind you?" he asked.

The scraping came again.

"Hey, what's that noise?" Dagger asked.

"That's why I'm asking you," Boggs said, finally turning completely and facing Dagger.

Boggs laid flat, and shone his headlamp between Dagger's legs. He peered deep into the section of the tunnel they'd just come from.

The scraping came louder this time, much louder. Almost as if whatever was making the noise was coming their way.

Boggs held his breath, listening to the commotion and preparing for the worst.

There always was the worst.

The scraping echoed down the tunnel now, like railroad carts grinding on metal. But in the mechanical (was it mechanical?) commotion, he heard something else, something alive.

Breathing.

Great, Boggs thought.

And like clockwork, the things whipped around the corner, and at last Boggs saw what they were: lerkas. With their hybrid crocodile snouts, shut closed with their tongues hanging out the side.

"Oh shit oh shit oh shit oh shit!" Dagger said, spinning a 180 and cracking his head into Boggs' head.

Boggs' world spun for a moment, but he was able to recover. He seized Dagger by his shirt, and managed to jam him past himself in the tunnel so that Boggs was the first to get attacked.

"We need to run," Dagger said.

Boggs shook his head as he fumbled with his pockets. He whipped out the lens-shaped device, and tossed it five feet ahead of him. Far down in the tunnel, eyes, snouts, and claws hurried their way, desperate and hungry.

Boggs seized the thumb drive device and clicked it, while forming two lasers in the air. Once they touched, a perimeter laser fence formed, but only on Boggs' open side, where it completely touched the tunnel's walls.

The lerkas kept coming.

"Hey," Dagger said. "That fucking Jekyll is back, sir!"

Boggs turned to look, and saw Jekyll thirty feet into the tunnel, cocking his head and emitting language inflections. Jekyll opened and clamped his mouth shut twice, and Boggs wondered if Jekyll was mocking them again.

Boggs turned back to the lerkas as they drew closer.

"Ready?" he said to Dagger as he raised his ZR-15.

"Always," Dagger said, following Boggs' lead.

Boggs leaned to the side against the tunnel wall, letting Dagger inch forward and to the right so both men could aim. Once in position, Boggs glanced back to see what Jekyll was up to. The animal just stared at him with its head cocked, and wagged its tail.

Dagger eyed Jekyll. "Thing fucking gives me the creeps," he said.

"Yeah," Boggs said. "But not as bad as what's coming. Fire."

The roar of gunfire in that narrow tunnel was deafening. The lead lerka took the brunt as expected, collapsing to the ground like a cased sausage.

But more came.

The men fired, taking out the next lead lerka with quick, efficient bursts. Boggs didn't feel remorse about killing this species after what they'd done to Dr. Mana. And in a way, the lerkas were tougher than the spitters. They'd have to be dealt with, sooner or later.

"We need to reduce ammo expenditure," Boggs said. "Let them come to the fence."

Dagger looked at him with incredulous eyes.

"We have to try it sometime," Boggs said. "Trust me."

The lerkas drew to within twenty feet, then ten feet, then five feet. The lead lerka burst into the fence and was sliced apart at the ankles, haunches, skull, and shoulders. Body parts and blood flew towards Dagger and Boggs, with nowhere to duck. The next lerka repeated the firsts' mistake. The third lerka realized what was happening, and slammed all four paws into the ground, sliding right up to the fence and growling inches from the lasers. A large scar ran down this lerka's forehead, and its face contained more definition than the others. Two more lerkas appeared behind this one, angling their snouts sideways and swaying them in the air, smelling the men and perhaps their loss of dinner.

For now.

"It fucking works," Dagger said. "Holy crap it works."

"On this round," Boggs said.

The remaining lerkas sniffed the air and swayed their snouts, then retreated down the tunnel from where they'd come.

Boggs wondered if the lerkas knew another way out, or if they were trapped down here.

"Let's go," Boggs said, leaving the laser fence up and crawling away, deeper into the tunnel.

"Shouldn't we take them out?" Dagger said.

"They're trapped," Boggs said.

"I don't know," Dagger said. "We might run into them again, sir."

"I doubt it," Boggs said. But he did have to wonder about that. For now, he just wanted to get the hell out of the tunnels. As the men crawled deeper into the darkness, the glowing green lasers hummed and illuminated their past. Ahead, the cackling calls of Jekyll echoed down the tunnels.

17.

Boggs and Dagger took a break, after what must've been two miles of tunnel. It was now clear to Boggs what exactly had made this tunnel. As they had drawn deeper and deeper into the depths, Boggs witnessed defined markings, no doubt caused by the intense burrowing of a giant worm, or at least a sub-adult giant worm.

But there didn't appear to be any recent activity, at all. Boggs wondered if perhaps they'd been led on a wild goose chase by the strange Jekyll. Either way, there was no turning around. Boggs clenched his fist and checked the battery level on his headlamp.

76% left.

Good, he thought.

In the semi-darkness of the tunnel, Dagger sipped on his nutrient straw. It reminded Boggs to do the same. He'd been running on empty, and survival wasn't all about running and gunning. There were scientific, biological concerns as well. If you didn't address those concerns, you couldn't do much else.

Boggs immediately felt better as he sucked on his nutrient straw. And the concoction contained turmeric, a potent anti-inflammatory herb. Boggs could feel his aches and pains fade ever so slightly, and that was enough for him to push forward.

"I'm not sure about this," Dagger said. "Feels like we're going deeper, not towards the surface."

Boggs shone his headlamp along the tunnel surface. "I think we've maintained our depth," he said. "With slight variations. We'll give it another few miles, and then make our way back, and kill the lerkas if we have to."

"We have no rope," Dagger said. "If we go back, we can't get out."

Boggs shook his head. "We won't have to go back," he said.

Boggs crawled deeper into the tunnel. He was worried that he hadn't seen Jekyll for a long time. Maybe the lerkas got him. Or something else.

Ha, he thought. *Right.*

After several more hours, Boggs at last saw a sliver of light the size of a pen far ahead.

"You see that?" Boggs said to Dagger.

"Oh hell yes I do," Dagger said, picking up his pace to the point he slammed into Boggs.

After a few minutes, the sliver of light bloomed, until the men were crouched under a mass of soil and rocks, not the usual smooth tunnel surface. Dagger started to claw his way through.

"Hold up," Boggs said. "You don't want to bring the whole thing down on us."

Boggs took Dagger's ZR-15 rifle, along with his own, and stood them on end. Then he crammed the two backpacks between the pointed barrels and the roof of the tunnel on both sides of them, forming two support pillars.

"Now we can dig," Boggs said.

The men carefully removed dirt and rocks, and sooner rather than later the thin slit of light blossomed, revealing grass and sky. Boggs formed two of his hands into a step that Dagger climbed onto with one foot, while Boggs pushed him through, making sure to keep his mouth shut so he didn't eat Mawholla.

Smiling at him from above, Dagger offered his hand. Boggs obliged, and soon the men were standing on the tundra again, breathing the pristine air.

Boggs took out the binoculars he'd stuffed into his pocket, and scanned the terrain. Far away, the CAV-117 rested, just a blur on the horizon. Boggs swung the binoculars towards Pine Tree Ridge. There, he saw something moving into the clump of trees.

"What is it?" Dagger asked.

"It's Jekyll," Boggs said. "He's going home."

Boggs shook his head, and hiked in the direction of the CAV. "And we should too."

18.

In the morning, Boggs, Dr. Tara, and Dagger returned to the place they'd exited the tunnel and recovered the rifles and gear using a system of ropes.

"That must've been fun," Dr. Tara said.

"Ball of laughs," Boggs said.

Dagger shook his head. "Hated every second of it," he said.

When they'd recovered all the gear, Dr. Tara handed anti-bacterial wipes to the men.

"We don't know everything about the soil yet," she said. "Dr. Volter and Dr. Reynolds are running soil composition samples at Base Camp One. Before we determine the precise composition, we need to take precautions."

"Jesus," Dagger said, taking a clump of soil and grinding it in his hands before flinging it into the air. "It's just like Earth's soil. So don't worry about the tests."

Dr. Tara sighed, and handed Dagger another anti-bacterial wipe. "I'm not asking," she said. "It's an order."

"Yes ma'am," Dagger said, taking the wipe and cleaning off his hands.

Boggs scanned the horizon with his binoculars, up towards Pine Tree Ridge. He did not catch movement this time, and wondered if Jekyll had finally left the area.

The CAV had been parked only fifty yards from their excavation point the previous night, and Boggs had Danni approach the tundra in stealth mode, running the engines at one quarter power. Boggs didn't want to risk another unnecessary and preventable lerka encounter.

The group shouldered daypacks and rifles, then hiked towards Pine Tree Ridge. Dr. Tara wanted samples from the trees, and to set out a few strands of barbed wire for collecting hair samples on whatever game trails they could find. This would not harm Mawholla's animals, only grab a quick bit of fur and maybe skin.

"They used to use this back in Glacier National Park, Montana, when it had grizzly bears," Dr. Tara said. "They'd get all kinds of hair samples, from the intended target, ranging from wolverines, lynx, and fishers. It's a neat way to collect samples."

Dagger coughed. "Yeah, I'm sure the critter feels it's real neat when barbed wire takes a chunk of its fur off."

Dr. Tara sighed. "They don't even realize it," she said. "Especially the bears. After Zobroksky's study in 2137, the repetition of pain wild animals go through is much, much more than what domesticated people experience. They develop a tolerance to bites, scratches, wounds, tooth infections and other injury. And this tolerance is passed down genetically. Whereas for people, we became more and more sheltered and home-dwelling, to the point where small injuries are no longer tolerated, and we passed that sensitivity along in our genes, too."

"So that's why we got so lazy and fat," Dagger said.

"That's not a politically correct, or nice way to say it," Dr. Tara said. "Yes, we are mostly an obese species. But not as obese as the human race was back at the turn of the millennium. Reduced food supplies made sure of that. But yes, in a sense."

The group finally reached Pine Tree Ridge, and began the low climb into the trees.

Dr. Tara pointed to a tree, and then had Boggs help her wrap a strand of barbed wire around it several times while Dagger kept watch.

Then Dr. Tara opened a small vial of something, and used a small paint brush to apply the scent to the barbed wire.

"It's a neutral pheromone," Dr. Tara said. "An attractant that won't infect Mawholla with invasive microbes. We have to be careful not to harm the native ecosystem balance."

Boggs shook his head. "We've already been pissing and shitting all over the planet," he said. "It's a little late for that."

Dr. Tara blushed. "That's a nice picture," she said. "Also, it's not enough to really cause any harm...yet. Once we get a few hundred people here, we're looking at a human system capable of starting to really impact the local environment."

Boggs stuffed what was left of the barbed wire strands into his backpack and headed further up the ridge. He glassed in every direction, expecting to see Jekyll trotting somewhere on the edge of the horizon, but the creature never appeared. A cool wind sighed through the trees, shaking them a little.

Dr. Tara's COMM device beeped, and she thumbed on the speaker so everyone could hear.

"Dr. Tara, this is Dr. Volter. Can you hear me?"

"Yes," Dr. Tara said. "Sam and Dagger are listening, too."

There was a pause, and some kind of racket over at Base Camp 1.

"We're having trouble with what you call the spitters," Dr. Volter said. "They're finding weaknesses in the fence, and then exploiting those weaknesses. I'm not sure how much time we have."

Boggs opened his COMM device and got Staunch on the line. "Hey," he said. "What the fuck is going on?"

Staunch seemed amused. "Portman and I have got it, sir," he said. "The biologists are overreacting."

"I heard that!" Dr. Volter said. "No one here is overreacting."

"We've already had this conversation," Staunch said to Dr. Volter. "We have it handled."

Boggs nodded. "Copy that. We were planning on heading back, once we set up the sample collection devices for Jekyll, and whatever else may rub against it."

"Over and out," Staunch said.

Boggs clicked off his COMM device and turned to Dr. Tara, who was still on the line with Dr. Volter. "My men have it taken care of," he said. "But we're still going to head back."

Before Dr. Tara could put her COMM device away, a flock of unusually large birds flew just above the crest of Pine Tree Ridge.

Boggs had a bad feeling. A really bad feeling.

"Go," he said, shoving Dr. Tara and Dagger down the ridge. "Just go."

As the three of them ran between the staggered trees downslope, a cloud of dust and grass emerged at the top of the ridge.

"Lerkas," Boggs said.

"Oh shit," Dagger said. "The ship is a long way off."

Boggs knew Dagger was right, but there was no choice. If they didn't make it, Boggs would deploy the emergency laser shield, and shoot the lerkas.

Except when he looked back, he realized there were now two dozen lerkas. Their hungry eyes glimmered in the sunlight, their composed snouts clamped shut, tongues stuck out the side.

He was getting so God damn sick of seeing them.

"How many frag grenades do you have?" Boggs asked as he ran.

"Five," Dagger said.

Boggs helped free Dr. Tara's leg from a cold spring, her boot making a viscous sucking sound as it pulled free of the muck.

"I've got four," Boggs said. "We're going to have to use them soon."

"Can't wait," Dagger said. "Tired of these fuckers."

Dr. Tara looked behind her, and stumbled again. Boggs seized her by the arm and propelled her forward. "You get used to it," he said.

Dr. Tara looked at him with horrified eyes. "Get used to what, the ice water or the lerkas?"

"Both," Boggs said.

Up ahead, the CAV-117 drew closer, but behind them, the lerkas did as well.

Boggs hated how they never opened their long snouts. This quiet, odd determination made his skin crawl.

And not much made his skin crawl.

"Dr. Tara," Boggs said, trying to catch his breath, "I'm going to count to three. When I hit three, I want you to keep running."

"Got it," Dr. Tara shouted in-between gasps for air.

"Dagger, when I hit three, I want you to stop, pull a frag nade, and then launch it at the lerkas in duality with me."

"Yes sir," Dagger said.

"One."

"Two."

"Three!"

Dr. Tara continued on her path towards the CAV, but Dagger and Boggs stopped in their tracks, each taking a frag grenade, pulling the pin, and chucking them a good fifty yards.

Boggs had been well-practiced. His grenade exploded in the air, about ten feet off the ground. Dagger's grenade thudded to the earth in a line-drive before exploding. Two of the lead lerkas shrieked in pain and spasmed on the ground until they went limp. The rest carried on, undeterred.

Boggs and Dagger let fly two more grenades, and this time Dagger's exploded eight feet off the ground, blowing apart a charging lerka's skull. At last the pack seemed to take notice that if they continued, their heads would be blown off too.

The lerkas slowed, then stopped. They stared eerily at Dagger and Boggs while raising their snouts in the air.

"Fuckin' stay," Dagger said.

The two men retreated, never turning their backs on the lerkas. They made it forty yards before the lerka pack came again, and Boggs let loose another frag grenade.

This time, the lerkas saw the grenade coming, and dispersed.

The blast did not affect them.

"Shit," Dagger said.

"Run," Boggs said.

Boggs and Dagger sprinted towards the CAV, reaching the ramp just before Dr. Tara slammed the button, drawing it closed behind them.

Boggs went to the console monitors and watched. There, not fifty feet from the CAV paced the pack of lerkas, staring at the ship with their clamped snouts.

"Fascinating specimens," Dr. Tara said as she dialed in the on-board video recorder.

"No," Dagger said. "*Creepy* specimens."

19.

The COMM light lit up on the CAV-117, and Boggs picked up the privacy line. It was Staunch, and he didn't seem happy.

"Something happened," he said, out of breath and uncharacteristically nervous.

And that bothered Boggs a lot.

A whole hell of a lot.

"Go ahead," Boggs said. "I'm not a fucking mind reader."

"It's Dr. Reynolds," Staunch said. "He was running soil samples at the laser fence perimeter, and now he's missing."

Boggs checked the outboard monitors on the CAV. The suns had already set, and darkness was creeping across Mawholla.

"When did he go missing?" Boggs asked, keeping his voice quiet from the others until he could figure out his plan of action.

"Can't say for sure, but he went out an hour ago," Staunch said.

"Why did he not have an armed escort?" Boggs asked.

"He was upset with us," Staunch said. "Said he wanted to go out on his own and conduct an experiment."

"Great," Boggs said. "Can you and Portman handle a rescue effort right now? We won't be in for another thirty minutes."

"We can, sir," Staunch said. "May we bring the Havoc 12?"

"Negative for now," Boggs said. "Dagger and I will follow your lead when we get back. I'll handle the Havoc 12."

"Yes sir," Staunch said. "And sir...I have a bad feeling about this one."

"Recon Elite runs on effectiveness, not feelings," Boggs said.

Staunch paused on the line, then spoke in a nervous voice, which shocked Boggs:

"Sir, when are reinforcements arriving?"

Boggs studied Dr. Tara, and the ship for a moment, how out of place they all seemed. He wondered if the sheer weight of the pristine, natural world of Mawholla had begun to press upon Staunch. The endless wilderness. The wild. What-was-not-Earth. It sure as hell was pressing on Boggs.

"Not for a couple months," Boggs said. "We're the tip of the spear. Figuratively, and literally."

"Okay," Staunch said. "Portman is securing our gear now. I'll keep you updated."

Boggs clicked off the COMM device, and turned to Dr. Tara. He cut right to the point.

"Dr. Reynolds went missing within the hour," he said.

Dr. Tara's mouth hung slack, and then she brought her hand to cover it. As she settled into the reality, her mouth closed and she balled her fingers into a fist.

"I understand," she said. "I don't like it, but I understand. This is how it's going to be. It's dangerous. Any one of us could be eaten, or killed, or fall off a cliff. The possibilities are endless."

Boggs nodded. "They are," he said. "We've got Staunch and Portman on a recovery mission right now. That leaves Dr. Volter alone on your CAV. You good with that?"

"Yes," Dr. Tara said. "Base Camp One is safe."

Boggs wasn't sure how all that safe Base Camp 1 was, but he didn't want to mess with Dr. Tara's emotions right now. His job was to be the steady hand, not an emotional whiner. And it was something that had always helped him in life when it came to the opposite sex, and bosses. No woman worth a damn ever wanted to date a whiner/complainer. And no one wanted that in a leader, either.

"Will be back in thirty minutes or so," Boggs said. "When we land, Dagger and I will be joining Staunch and Portman on the mission to find Dr. Reynolds."

"Good," Dr. Tara said. "I have faith you'll find him."

20.

Dagger already had the gear ready by the time they landed. Boggs escorted Dr. Tara up into the CAV-121, then met Dagger at the base of the ramp.

Boggs pulled out a laser bending device known as "Little Beaver", and pushed the button while aiming it at the northwest corner of the fence. A second later, four layers of laser fencing contorted, forming a man-sized hole. Dagger quickly snuck through, and Boggs followed. As soon as he did, his COMM device beeped. Before answering, Boggs closed the fresh hole.

Then he put the COMM in silent mode. The spitters seemed to have excellent hearing.

"Staunch here."

"Go ahead, Staunch."

"We haven't found a damn thing yet," Staunch said quietly as weird bird song cried out on the COMM device. Wherever Staunch and Portman had gone, it sounded like they were deep in the wilderness.

Then again, the entire planet was deep wilderness.

"Nothing, no sign, no trace?"

"No sir," Staunch said. "We've covered all four sides of the fence, spread out in two hundred yard sections, each side."

"Odd," Boggs said. "Let's push out to four hundred yards, forming perimeters. We'll stay in two groups to cover more ground."

"Roger that," Staunch said. "Do you have the Havoc 12?"

"Yes," Boggs said. He wondered for a moment about firing the Havoc so close to the CAVs, and Base Camp 1. And he wondered about that tiny, but glaring failure percentage admitted by CPB weapons engineers.

"Let's just hope we don't have to use it," Boggs said.

Boggs and Dagger walked carefully through the old growth rainforest. Every sound, every twitch of branch spiked adrenaline through him. He thought he heard spitters growling and hissing just out of sight, and checked his LifeForm device just to be sure.

All good.

For now.

The only things showing on the device were small weasel-like creatures, and a variety of bird species, all deemed "neutral".

Still, Boggs didn't like it.

He reached into his pack and unfolded a portable drone, then flung it into the air.

"Nice," Dagger said.

A moment later the LifeForm beeped, revealing that it had established connection with the drone. No scan needed. The biologists had made welcome modifications.

Boggs crouched in the dark forest, watching the drone as it hovered below the vast canopy. Mawholla's lone moon cast an eerie glow against tree trunks that simply had to be seen to be believed.

Boggs checked his LifeForm meter. The drone picked up squirrel animals as they scurried away from it, and a couple owl-like species.

"Come on," Boggs said.

The two men stalked a hundred yards into the wilderness. Boggs' COMM device vibrated in his pocket, and he held the device to his ear.

"Staunch here," the voice said.

"Go ahead," Boggs said.

"Nothing except small neutral animals," Staunch said. "And no Dr. Reynolds. Not even a trace of blood, or a shoe, or anything."

"Same over here," Boggs said. He paused for a moment, thinking of his next plan. It was pretty simple. "Let's push out another two hundred yards," he said. "I'm not giving up yet."

"Roger that," Staunch said.

Boggs carefully clicked off the COMM device, and checked the LifeForm meter. The drone had reached 150 yards ahead of them, and was beaming back no hostile species.

"Let's move," Boggs said, hoisting the Havoc 12 over his shoulder.

Dagger lit a cigarette, and cupped his hands over the flame.

"Put that fucking thing out," Boggs said. "That cherry is like a spotlight."

Dagger pinched off the tobacco end, and pocketed the filter.

"Shit habit," Boggs said. "Slows you down."

"Yes sir," Dagger said, as he followed Boggs deeper into the forest.

Above, moonlight gleamed on the cracked bark of trees perhaps a thousand years old, maybe more. Below, Boggs scoured the ground for any sign of Dr. Reynolds: drag marks, a piece of bootlace, a torn patch of fabric.

But there was nothing except for the spongy forest floor, the fallen giants, and the occasional head-high fern.

The LifeForm device beeped.

Boggs looked down at the screen, and his heart pumped a couple beats faster.

The drone beamed back a *new* creature, deemed as hostile. The creature ran side to side, like a football running back, and then disappeared out of the drone's range.

The forest fell eerily silent, even the squirrels and birds had quieted, revealing only the moonlight slanting down through the canopy upon the humongous grooved tree bark, like so many highways.

Boggs held his hand out to Dagger, and both men stopped and analyzed their surroundings, not saying a word.

The silence of Mawholla's wilderness overcame them like a tidal wave, the sheer power and magnitude of which the men had never felt before.

To the north, a branch snapped.

"Shit," Dagger whispered. "You hear that?"

Boggs nodded, and raised his Havoc 12. He had a strong feeling it was time.

Thirty yards out, another branch snap.

The LifeForm beeped, revealing the hostile creature once more. Before Boggs could make out its complete shape on the screen, the creature evaded the drone's camera.

Another snap, twenty yards out.

Boggs knelt, and waved Dagger down with him.

The animal emerged from a patch of ferns, its face a twisting, convoluted mess. Boggs had never seen anything like it on Mawholla. The thing actually had two faces, like two hairless boars stuck together, tusks and all. But it moved like a spider, skittering, juking, pausing momentarily, then skittering again. Its legs were crab-like, yet covered in thick hair on the top sides.

Four pairs of eyes stared intently in the direction of Boggs and Dagger. The creature processed the scene, sniffed the air, and leapt forward all at once, showing a remarkable amount of dexterity and mental ability.

"Nade," Boggs said.

Dagger let loose a frag grenade, which exploded five feet off the ground. The creature turned its two heads sideways, and absorbed the blast with a bizarre shield-like head plate that Boggs hadn't seen before, because it angled down over the back of the thing's neck.

And still, it came for them.

The LifeForm beeped again, this time showing another creature further back in the woods, and then another and another.

"Holy shit," Dagger said. "We're fucked."

Boggs reached for his COMM device. "Staunch, fixate on my coordinates and get your asses over here."

"Yes sir," Staunch said.

Dagger opened fire on the creature with his rifle, inflicting serious damage to its legs, which seemed to be its weak spot. The thing crumpled into the ground, then chewed its own injured leg off, and came at the men again.

Dagger launched another frag nade, and it exploded too close to the men, knocking them back and ringing their ears.

Boggs looked around drunkenly and wobbled to his feet, making sure to keep a steady grip on the Havoc 12 despite all else.

Dagger fell backwards into a log, knocking himself out cold.

One half of the creature's two faces had been blown clean off by the frag nade, leaving an eye dangling by a tenuous thread of sinew. Its mouth opened, revealing hippo-like tusks and a tongue that was padded with teeth pointing inward.

Cute, Boggs thought.

Behind the creature, more emerged, scraping their legs together and turning their heads 180 degrees to show off the neck armor. They confused Boggs, because the two faces made it seem like a lot more were present.

After a brief pause, the creatures leapt towards Boggs, grunting and drooling a viscous fluid. Boggs hoped these weren't the poisonous spitter variety.

But they were, of course.

The was Mawholla's specialty.

Before the creatures could rear back and spit, gunfire erupted from the east. Boggs turned in time to see Staunch and Portman, kneeling and power-attacking with everything they had in their arsenal.

Dagger woke up, shook it off, and hurled a frag nade, which imploded ten feet in the air, roughly three feet above the creatures' heads.

Four of them collapsed and rolled onto their backs, feet kicking the air like a dog held above water. The venom they were about to spit shot up in the air, and came down on their grotesque heads. The creatures screamed.

Boggs was getting tired of the venom.

Really tired.

Six more creatures scurried in from the west, clicking and grunting as they wetted their mouths, no doubt prepping their venom.

Boggs kneeled and aimed the Havoc 12 in the direction of the largest pack of creatures. The LCD readout confirmed the LifeForm signature, and the bullet exited the tube at half speed, as if assessing which path would be the absolute deadliest and most destructive.

A half second later, it found its path. Rather than puncturing the first lead creature at 12 o'clock, it veered left, and punched itself through the brains of two creatures at 9 o'clock.

But Boggs wondered if the Havoc 12 engineers had ever planned for creatures with two heads. Because killing one of the damn things wasn't going to be enough.

And did the creatures have two hearts as well? Maybe to make sure there was enough oxygen to keep those heads functioning at optimal levels.

The Havoc bullet passed through several heads, but it didn't kill all of the heads. The result was one head going limp and lolling, while the other head would turn red with all that extra blood no longer going to the damaged head, and the things would rage like mother fuckers.

As Dagger and Staunch emptied the ZR-15s into what was left of the creatures, Portman lobbed frag nades expertly, exploding them at the creatures' head level.

Smoke filled the air, mixing with blood, guts, bits of tree trunks and ferns, and the flinging venom that just kept missing Boggs and his men.

The creatures took a hell of a lot of punishment, ate bullets like a kid eats cotton candy. The Havoc 12 changed paths, cutting out the creatures' legs, leaving them limbless and squealing and shooting venom everywhere.

This moment of severity allowed Recon Elite to finish them off.

In all the commotion, Boggs' LifeForm meter beeped again.

Oh shit, he thought, knowing full well what it was. All the noise had attracted the spitters.

After the last grenade took out the only fully functioning creature, Boggs ordered his men to retreat to Base Camp 1.

Recon Elite retreated as carefully as they could, as several limping and spitting creatures tried to come at them. But the Havoc 12 bullet was too efficient, too deadly. It killed the last three, this time making sure to exit the first head at a hard angle so it could penetrate the second head.

Boggs was impressed. But he was also beat to shit. His age, and the level of action on Mawholla was wearing him down. He and his men needed rest. They'd given too much, lost too much.

In the distance, Boggs caught the glow of the laser fence. Ahead of him, Staunch, Dagger, and Portman made good time, with Staunch checking back every so often to make sure Boggs was okay.

Boggs fished the fence bending device out of his pocket, and then realized he wouldn't need it. There was already a hole in the fence, enough for a medium sized spitter to get through.

His men looked at him like ghosts.

"Must've malfunctioned," Boggs said, hurrying through the hole and back to the CAV. "Staunch, you come with me. Dagger and Portman, watch the fence breach."

"Yes sir," Dagger said.

Boggs raced back to CAV-121, only to learn that Dr. Tara and Dr. Volter were perfectly fine.

And all at once, Boggs understood.

There'd been a fence malfunction, shortly before Dr. Reynolds had entered the yard alone. Something had entered, possibly one of the newer creatures they'd just encountered (most likely), and seized the doctor, dragging him into the woods.

Dr. Tara grabbed Boggs by the arm.

"Did you find him?" she asked.

Boggs shook his head. "Not a trace."

Dr. Volter pursed his lips, and stared back down at his lab samples. He was strangely, much calmer than Dr. Tara.

"You said you'd find him, Sam," she said.

"It's not over yet," Boggs lied. "It's not safe out there. We encountered a new species and ran into trouble."

Boggs described the new species to her, and handed Dr. Tara his LifeForm device. She connected it into the onboard diagnostics. A moment later a series of images along with a biological imprint appeared on the center console.

Dr. Tara tried to explain some of the features, but Boggs was worried about his men.

Dr. Tara tossed Boggs a fence repair kit, and he headed back out into the Mawholla night with Staunch.

Dagger and Portman were waiting for him at the fence breach, ZR-15s aimed at the hole.

"We heard something out there," Dagger said. "Not sure what the hell it was."

Boggs had made the mistake of leaving his LifeForm back on the ship for Dr. Tara.

He kneeled, and aimed the fence repair wand, connecting lasers that had failed to connect. It was trippy to Boggs, almost magical, and he felt surreal doing it. But in a minute the work was done, and the perimeter laser fence for Base Camp 1 was back to functioning 100%.

"Nice work," Portman said, stealing a cigarette from Dagger and lighting up. "But what about the missing doctor?"

"Morning," Boggs said. "Dr. Tara may have hinted at the fact the new species are nocturnal. If that's the case, we're much better off continuing the mission at sunrise."

Dagger shook his head. "Come on man," he said. "You know Dr. Reynolds is crab dinner right now."

A well of anger bubbled up inside Boggs. "We don't know for certain," he said. "Dr. Reynolds could've been curious and wandered through the breach, and became lost. He might still be out there, just waiting for us to not be Negative Nancy's, and to get the job fucking done."

Portman nodded. "I agree with that. It's what we do. We're Recon Elite, not a bunch of fucking pussies."

"Yeah," Staunch said, taking a sip from his nutrient straw and belching. "Dr. Reynolds is a smart son of a bitch. He'll know to hole up, and not run around out in the wilderness like a chicken with his neck cut off."

I hope that's true, Boggs thought. He put on a good show for his men, but deep down, he had a feeling Dr. Reynolds was as dead as that giant worm up in the tundra.

"It's not a democracy," Boggs said. "At least not for the tip of the spear. But I like your spirit, men."

With the fence repaired, Boggs headed back to CAV-117. It was time to rest. As soon as he laid in his bunk, he fell asleep and dreamed of Dr. Tara. He dreamt she was native to Mawholla, and had snakes growing out of her long, feminine hair, and that these snakes connected to branches and vines in the old growth forest. As Dr. Tara spread herself amongst the trees, she laughed a twisted laugh, her eyes like roiling oceans. Boggs muttered in his sleep, tossing and turning. Eventually he calmed, and slipped into blackness.

21.

They awoke in the morning, shouldered their gear, and created a fresh hole in the Base Camp 1 security fence. Boggs ordered Dagger and Portman to head south, while he and Staunch headed north. After several miles, they were to double back, and then branch out from the eastern fence, while Dagger and Portman branched out from the western. They were to repeat this for several hours, and then push further into the wilderness. But this time, instead of doubling back, they'd conduct a 360 degree search several miles out, and slowly tighten the noose around Base Camp 1 in a pincer movement.

It was a good plan.

Boggs and Staunch had snuck coffee into the nutrient straws in the morning, enjoying the crystalline high and the extra edge of energy.

Boggs had to admit he felt good. He'd finally had a decent night's sleep, and he was going to complete this mission today, regardless of whether the ending was happy or not.

The woods were especially eerie this morning, thick with dew, the calls of birds and squirrels hushed by low fog that made visibility questionable at best.

But still they made it a mile out.

And no sign of Dr. Reynolds, not even tracks.

But there were plenty of other tracks, ranging from tiny rabbit-like imprints to much bigger animals that no human had ever seen before.

It appeared, as usual, that Mawholla was much thicker with wildlife than the original drones had discovered. The terrain was simply too varied, too thick, and too impenetrable to get reliable readings. And it was here, in this ancient forest that beasts wandered.

Boggs clutched his LifeForm in his right hand, thankful for the equipment. Where would they be without this invention by one of the chief engineers at CPB?

Nowhere.

They'd be worm meal, dead, rotting, food for something here, or infected on one of the other planets, never even making it to Mawholla.

The LifeForm beeped in Boggs' hand, indicating an animal dead ahead.

Before he could ascertain what kind of creature it was, the thing darted through the fog off to their left, grunting profusely. Staunch went to fire, but Boggs palmed down his rifle barrel.

The LifeForm beeped back that the creature was neutral.

It looked like a big hairy pig to Boggs, and it was possibly rooting around the woodland for grubs and other bugs to devour. The animal showed absolutely no interest in them. But Boggs COMM'ed Dagger and Portman anyway, and warned them a big animal was rummaging through their perimeter.

Eventually, the sound of breaking branches faded, and the pig cleared their area. This was important to Boggs, because he didn't want a neutral, noisome animal obscuring the sounds of an animal that might be far more dangerous: especially in this thick fog.

Once the sounds faded, Boggs and Staunch proceeded further north, up a steep hill embedded with ankle-breaking boulders. Everything was slick and moist, and Boggs slipped several times, catching himself at the last minute. The jungle was thick here, the smell of rotting soil and fat greens filling his nostrils.Plump, awkward birds flapped up into the canopy from the understory, leaving long white strands of shit as they flew. Squirrel-like animals chittered and dropped seed-cones upon the men, just missing their heads.

Here and there the thick fog revealed and opened, where rays from the two suns lit up motes and various insect forms. And this worried Boggs the most.

He stopped and retrieved a can of DEET bug spray from his backpack, and applied it to himself and Staunch. As the day warmed, Boggs had noticed the bugs becoming more and more numerous, to the point they were landing on their skin. And no one, not even the biologists had any clue what these insects could do. For all Boggs knew, one bite would be instant paralysis, or some other horrific effect. He'd studied poisonous insects on Earth for his own personal knowledge, and the sheer amount of them was staggering. So why would Mawholla be any different?

Staunch coughed as he accidentally sprayed some of the DEET into his mouth.

"Nice shot," Boggs said as thick fog encased the men on their climb up Buggy Peak.

Boggs looked down at his feet, and noticed a fat centipede scurrying across his boot, its torso ribbed with thick tubes. Before he could take another step, a Gila-lizard like creature shot out from a rock and seized the centipede by its midsection, biting down hard and shooting guts out the side. The centipede thrashed, but the bigger creature worked its jaws like scissors, and soon had the entire centipede in its mouth minus a couple back legs. The creature regarded Boggs with a condescending eye, then slithered back into a crevasse in the rocks.

"Wicked," Staunch said as he sipped on his nutrient straw.

Boggs kicked the centipede guts off his boot, and continued to climb, keeping an ever watchful eye on anything else that might surprise them from the rocks.

Enormous, untouched trees punched through the fog, some of them laying crisscrossed across a moss-covered gorge. Far below and out of sight, a river roared and piped through a slot canyon. A creature stared back at the men from atop one of the crisscrossed logs.

A bird for sure, Boggs thought.

It looked like an eagle, but even bigger. It watched the men with untrusting eyes, then turned its head to the side and unfolded its wings. It leapt off the log and soared down into the gorge, thick fog curling off its wingtips. Boggs blinked, and the majestic bird was gone.

"Fucking cool," Staunch said.

Boggs agreed, but something was bothering him.

He looked down at his LifeForm meter, and wondered why it hadn't beeped for the lizard animal, and this eagle.

The answer to that was readily apparent: It wasn't working. The screen simply wouldn't come on. Boggs thumbed the power switch off and on, but no luck. He shook it a bit (the tried and true meathead method), no luck either.

He had the urge to chuck the thing into the gorge, but that was impulsive alternate-reality Sam Boggs, not the emotionally-centered Sam Boggs who ran Recon Elite Six.

Damn, he thought to himself, trying to hide his concern from Staunch. But Staunch was no fool.

"Fuck it," Staunch said. "We have eyes and ears."

"Excellent point," Boggs said. Maybe they'd been too reliant on the LifeForm anyway. Maybe it was time to improve their natural skillset, and to start merging with Mawholla instead of being so damn clinical and reliant on technology.

Boggs packed away the LifeForm, and pushed onward. Staunch followed him, slipping occasionally on the mossy rocks that littered the gorge lips. Boggs shook his head, wondering if one of these times, Staunch was just going to plunge off the side.

"Easy killer," Boggs said. "We don't need to lose another."

Staunch frowned. "I'm an artist at this shit," he said. "Don't always show it, but I am."

The men continued hiking uphill, through the ancient trees. Even more crossed the gorge here, forming slick natural bridges.

Boggs glanced over at a particularly large fallen log, and paused.

Something lay atop the log, smack above the middle of the ravine. A white-colored something, sticking out like a white flag of surrender.

Boggs took out his binoculars and zeroed in on the item despite the thick fog.

It was Dr. Reynolds' jacket. He was sure of it.

"Well shit," Staunch said, setting his rifle down and climbing onto the log, slipping down as he failed to find sturdy purchase.

"Careful," Boggs said.

"I got it," Staunch said.

Staunch moved further out, holding his arms wide for balance, then bent down and grabbed the jacket.

"Well," Staunch said. "It sure as hell couldn't be anyone else's. And there's blood on it."

Staunch turned to toss the jacket at Boggs, but in doing so, he slipped. The jacket fluttered into the ravine and disappeared into the fog. Staunch was able to grasp onto a broken limb with his bare hand, but he didn't have long. The son of a bitch swayed there, a living pendulum.

"Good day for a swim," Staunch joked.

Boggs scrambled atop the fallen log, then sprinted out above the gorge, before leaping head first and seizing Staunch's free hand. Boggs dug his boot toes into the spongy moss, and was able to get enough traction to pull his friend onto the giant log. As the two men laid on their backs and gasped for breath, the unseen river below roared back up to them, as if angry at being robbed of its first human victim.

"You have to be more careful," Boggs said as he rose to his feet. "No more showing off. Pull your head out of your ass."

"Yes sir," Staunch said.

Boggs helped Staunch up, and gave him a swat on the shoulder. "Go get our rifles," he said. "And let's see what's on the other side of this gorge."

22.

By the time the two men crossed the gorge and entered the woods, the fog had thickened, puffs of it wafting out between the sentinel trees.

Boggs took out his COMM device.

"We found Dr. Reynolds' jacket," he said. "Get your asses up here. We're on the western side of the ravine, in what we're calling The Lost River."

"Roger that," Portman said. "We encountered a lone spitter moments ago, did not fire because it did not attack. Maybe they learned their lesson," Portman said.

"It's possible," Boggs said.

"We just got a fix on your location," Portman said. "See you in a few."

Boggs clicked off his COMM device, and sipped his nutrient straw. Then he checked his ZR-15, making sure it was loaded and clean. Staunch followed his lead, and then the two men hunkered down and waited for what was left of Recon Elite.

Boggs blinked and watched the foggy forest. As they sat there silent, the forest oozed to life around them. Numerous bird species cut through the fog, most with shorter wings and big, fanning tail feathers for maneuverability under the canopy. The squirrel-like creatures appeared often, bulging their eyes as they made territorial cries at the men, and other squirrels.

Boggs heard the sound of claws ripping up bark, and the squirrels disappeared. A bizarre animal appeared sideways on a tree, clinging to it as if it was no big deal at all. The thing had a long snout like an anteater, except this snout was lined with tiny teeth perfect for gripping a struggling squirrel. Boggs couldn't help but admire that the thing's teeth were angled backwards, so that struggling prey clamped in its jaws would only impale itself. Boggs admired effective, minimalistic weapons, and there was no doubt this new creature was the perfect squirrel killer. Boggs also knew he didn't need the LifeForm meter to understand the creature wasn't problematic for humans.

He relaxed a little, letting his shoulders down. As he did, a roar erupted deep in the forest.

Relaxation time was over.

"Spitter for sure," Staunch said.

Boggs nodded and listened as two more roars emitted from the foggy woods.

They sounded a hell of a lot closer.

Boggs stood, crunching a rock under his boot. For the briefest of moments, he thought he heard a man scream from the north.

"Hear that?" he asked Staunch.

"You bet your ass I did," Staunch said. "Can only be one thing."

The man screamed again, and Boggs realized it was Dr. Reynolds.

Boggs spoke into his COMM device, and informed Portman they were heading north from the original position. Then Boggs and Staunch hiked between tree trunks the size of houses, as ferns as big as their heads brushed against them. With every step, Boggs' boots sunk a few inches into the spongy, rotting forest floor.

Dr. Reynolds screamed again, a maddening plea for mercy more than anything.

Boggs put a finger to his pursed lips and turned to Staunch as he stepped forward into the fog. He estimated visibility at twenty yards, tops.

Dr. Reynolds cried out in pain. A shiver crept up Boggs' arms. The doctor was right there amongst them. But he could not see him. Not yet, anyway.

Staunch caught up to Boggs and tapped him on the shoulder. Boggs didn't care for the wild look in his eyes.

Dr. Reynolds cried out again, and this time Boggs honed in on the sound. Slowly the doctor came into view, but Boggs refused to believe what he was seeing. The doctor had been impaled onto a broken limb that jutted out from an enormous trunk. It punched through his body right at the hip bone, which must have caused unbelievable pain.

Boggs realized there was nothing that could be done. The LifeChambers would have zero positive effect on this kind of injury.

Dr. Reynolds squirmed on the branch, blood oozing down his leg in crimson ropes. The kind of blood that was dark and rich, coming from near the heart, and fast.

Unbelievably, Dr. Reynolds tried to speak:

"It's..." he said, struggling to speak as blood seeped from his wound. "It's a t-t-t-rap."

Before Boggs could fully pull his mind away from how Dr. Reynolds looked and focus on what the doctor was saying, something lunged at him from the fog, something big.

"Fucking spitters," Staunch shouted.

Boggs fired immediately, lighting up the fog in intense muzzle flashes. He aimed for the spitter's head, not its heart. The bullets tore into the target, which stood at least several feet higher than him.

To his left, another spitter ambushed Staunch, who turned to fire. But the spitter was too fast, and Staunch had made the deadly mistake of aiming for the body. The spitter released a torrent of venom, and it slathered Staunch's face as if he were dipped in it.

Boggs turned and fired at the second spitter, aiming for the jaws. Chunks of bone and flesh splattered into the air. Then Boggs pulled a frag nade, pulled the pin with his teeth and backhanded the nade into the air behind him. The nade exploded powerfully in the thick fog, knocking Boggs forward. The first injured spitter screeched unseen in the mist.

Boggs unloaded on the spitter that had gotten Staunch, pushing it deeper into the foggy woods. Then he knelt down and tended to his wounded man.

But the Staunch that Boggs had known for ten years was no more. He'd been replaced by a faceless, melting apparition, only recognizable by the clothing and American flag arm tattoo. Staunch shuddered and shook, and what was left of his mouth blew venom bubbles, before he stopped moving entirely.

Boggs stood and fired several rounds into Dr. Reynolds.

As the last gunshot echoes dissipated, Boggs heard other spitters stomping and trotting in the fog, no doubt about to redouble their efforts.

Boggs was stunned. He'd had no idea spitters would be capable of devising a trap like this, using men like bait to lure other men. A smaller one must have snuck in through the damaged fence and grabbed Dr. Reynolds.

Boggs was pissed at himself. All those hours they let the spitters watch them from the forest at Base Camp 1, thinking they were safe thanks to the laser fence. But the spitters and the big mommas had been scheming, waiting for just the right moment.

Boggs retreated from where he'd come, just as his COMM device vibrated in silent mode. He told Portman and Dagger to meet him at the original location, and that spitters were active in the northern quadrant.

Boggs stumbled across the gorge along the ancient log, doing his best to contain his emotions. He'd just seen his longtime friend turn into a ghoulish, disfigured thing that bore no resemblance to the man he'd known. And the pain must have been so severe, Staunch didn't even have time to cry.

That's what troubled Boggs the most. He tried to push away the mental pain, the shock, the anguish and the sudden loss. But he also tried to figure out how the spitter had seen Staunch so well in the thick fog…well enough to induce a devastating blow.

As Boggs scrambled across the log, the eagle-like bird soared below him, its wingspan unbelievably wide, before it disappeared into the fog deep in the ravine.

When Boggs reached the other side, Portman and Dagger were waiting for him.

"Where's Staunch?" Portman asked.

Boggs shook his head.

"Fuck that," Portman said. "Tell me you're joking."

"I'm sorry," Boggs said.

Dagger looked like he'd just been told he had a week to live. Maybe he did.

"Fuck this," Dagger said. "We're not equipped for spitters. We're just not. We don't have the type of goggles and helmets that can even block that shit."

"I'm not sure much can," Boggs said, "short of solid metal. Dr. Tara will have some answers for us."

"Oh will she?" Dagger said as he nervously surveyed the forest around him. "Unless she has some kind of miracle weapon, or fucking super helmets, I don't think she'll have a worthwhile answer."

Portman spat, and checked his ZR-15. "And Dr. Reynolds?" he asked.

Boggs wanted to hold back, to not tell his men about the gruesome scene. But that would be doing them a disservice, and possibly compromising their safety. They needed to know how intelligent the spitters were, and they needed to know now. Boggs crouched into the moss covered rocks near the gorge's edge, and spoke in a low, calm tone:

"They used him as bait," Boggs said. "To lure us in. They hit fast. Staunch fought bravely, but he got the smarter, faster spitter."

"Wait a fucking second," Dagger said. "You mean to tell me that those spitters took Dr. Reynolds hostage, and then used him to attract us?"

"Yes," Boggs said. "I can't put it any more simply."

"How did they keep him?" Dagger asked as he glanced around the woods.

"They had him on a broken limb," Boggs said.

"Did he suffer?" Portman asked.

"No," Boggs said. "When Staunch and I arrived, we ascertained he sustained a mortal injury that our automated systems couldn't heal. He tried to tell us it was a trap, and then we were hit on both sides. The venom got Staunch, and when he was gone, I made sure Dr. Reynolds wouldn't suffer."

"Awful," Portman said. "Could that be any more fucked up."

Boggs shook his head. "I've never seen anything like it." Boggs stood, and put a finger to his pursed lips. He thought he heard something across the ravine, something big moving through the woods.

The men turned and stared at the area where the ancient fallen log met the other side.

Slowly, as if emerging from some nightmare fever dream, a spitter materialized. It stared back at the men with knowing eyes, its long snake tail a mere shadow flicking deep in the fog. Its front arms and claws were slathered in blood.

Dagger opened fire, lighting up the ancient log and the foggy woods. The spitter hissed and retreated back into the mist, becoming nothing more than a blurry outline stalking the forest.

Portman and Dagger tossed frag nades, but the thick tree trunks bounced the nades back into the ravine, where they exploded mid-air. The concussion roared against the cliffs, shucking loose hunks of rock that tumbled unseen into the foggy maw. Something groaned down there in response to the disturbance.

Dagger gazed down into the chasm, wide-eyed. "What the fuck just made that noise?" he asked.

"Come on," Boggs said. "We're heading back."

"I want that spitter dead," Dagger said.

"We don't have home field advantage," Boggs said. "Recon Elite fights tough, but we fight smart, too. Let's get our asses back to camp. We need to inform Dr. Tara and Dr. Volter of our situation."

"We need the Havoc 12," Dagger said.

"That's on the list," Boggs said.

The three men made their way through the forest of giants, Boggs doing his best to keep his emotions in check. But when the men weren't looking, Boggs turned and glanced back from where they'd come from. "Goodbye old friend," he said.

23.

"It's made of a substance I've never seen before," Dr. Tara said. "The closest I've seen is capsaicinoids."

"Capsaicinoids?" Dagger asked.

"Yes. From the chili pepper back on earth. An extreme irritant to mammals. But this is an especially condensed and powerful version of it. It's used in mace and bear spray back on Earth. It stings the eyes, irritates the lungs so attackers are immobilized. But this version on Mawholla is so much more potent, to the point it eats right through skin and plastic. Even heavy plastics and some metal."

"It's the bane of our existence," Boggs said. "Literally."

"You're going to need metal helmets, metal gloves, and wrap-around goggles at least several inches thick to protect you from this."

Dagger scoffed. "I ain't wearing that shit," he said. "Slows you down, can't see shit."

Portman frowned, and jabbed a meaty finger into Dagger's chest. "Would you rather see 'just okay', or be completely blind from having your eyes burned out of your skull?"

Dagger grinded his teeth. "That's the thing," he said. "Wearing all that shit makes it more likely you'll get a super chili pepper kiss."

Boggs turned to Dr. Tara. "Do we have the necessary means to manufacture the equipment you suggest?" Boggs asked.

Dr. Tara paused, then spoke bluntly: "No," she said. "But I can message CPB and have them begin production on appropriate equipment."

"Awesome," Dagger said. "So what do we do until that happens? Could be months away."

"It will be prioritized," Dr. Tara said. "They'll send a small cargo ship."

Boggs nodded. "We'll make do until then," he said.

Dr. Tara studied the computer console, a puzzled look on her face.

"I've run habitat scans, and biological scans," she said. "Of all of the species you've countered so far, the lerkas, spitters, and crab-like creatures are the most hostile to our colonization of Mawholla. At this point, I'm advocating for the removal of the spitters from the planet. The lerkas and crabs are pending further review."

"How many are there?" Boggs asked.

"Impossible to say. Perhaps millions. Of course, you and your men won't be able to handle all of this one, Sam. Dr. Volter and I will engineer a DNA-penetrating virus sample that will affect only them."

Boggs had heard all this before. CPB biologists had done the same thing for crops, but the side effects of the pesticide had killed off bees and other critical pollinators. He wondered what effect this would have on the rest of Mawholla's wildlife, and in turn, what effect that would have on people.

"What about side effects?" Boggs asked.

"Highly unlikely," Dr. Tara said.

Dr. Volter concurred. "I've been working on a spitter DNA virus since first landing at Base Camp 1. I've run through all the variables."

Dr. Volter went into a sealed refrigerator, and pulled out a needle with a feathered end.

A dart gun needle.

Then Dr. Volter reached under the lab table, and procured a dart gun. "They have a soft spot just under their jaws," he said, holding up the gun and dart. "Try to get a good shot. All you need is to infect one, and they will pass the virus to each other."

"Why don't you be the one to shoot 'em?" Dagger said.

"That's your area of expertise," Dr. Volter said.

"You are out of line," Boggs said to Dagger, raising a finger at him. "These people are here to help. They do their job, we do our job. And when both of us do our jobs well, we save humanity. Get it?"

Dagger puffed his chest out and saluted Boggs. "Yes sir!" he said.

"Good," Boggs said.

24.

Boggs woke in the night and stumbled over to the security monitor. He saw his reflection in it, his hair growing scraggly, his five o'clock shadow growing deeper and richer, with specks of grey.

He flipped on the monitor and watched. As the screen flickered and auto-adjusted, something watched him, too. A spitter stood inches from the laser fence, cocking its head to the side.

"Come on boy," Boggs said. "Touch the fence, see how you feel."

Boggs put his boots on, grabbed the dart gun and loaded the dart. Then he lowered the ramp and headed straight for the spitter.

It saw him and waited a few seconds, then sniffed the air and bolted out of sight into the forest.

Boggs sighed. It had sensed something different. Maybe it was his lack of clothing. Maybe it was the dart gun. Whatever it was, the spitters had shown a disturbing level of intelligence.

Boggs went back into the CAV-117, and sat in the console chair, watching the monitors with the dart gun laid across his lap.

He drifted in and out of sleep, his eyes opening and revealing the monitor, sometimes watching as the feed twitched, faded and then stabilized. A few times he thought he glimpsed a big momma out there, watching and waiting.

In his random sleep, he thought of Sarah and Connor, running through the tundra zone of Mawholla, the two suns lighting up their faces. There were no lerkas, no worms, only safe, non-hazardous life forms. He thought of other things too, things he wished he didn't think of any more, like an animal silhouette on a distant horizon, angling away from the view of his binoculars, always just out of reach.

Jekyll.

He of the fastest legs Boggs had ever seen. The Blur Wizard, appearing for a nanosecond, and yet gone again just as fast. He wondered what that son of a bitch was up to. The trickster, the one who led them down the worm tunnel to safety, and then disappeared. Why would Jekyll do that after what they'd tried to do to him? Just a few Earthly meatheads unloading bullets at something they didn't grasp fully.

Had anything really changed?

And that's where Boggs was concerned the most. He knew it was likely he'd die. The tip of the spear was just that: the tip. Reinforcements wouldn't be here for two more months. The CAVs they flew were the first of their breed. So not only was Recon Elite and the biologists the tip of the sphere within a humanity context, the CAVs were the tip of the spear in the engineering context.

They were alone.

The good news was the biologist's CAV was reinforced with a year's supplies. And at some point Boggs and what was left of his men would establish a bona fide camp. But right now, the thick steel hull of the CAVs felt like the place to be.

In and out of sleep, Boggs' mind went back to Dr. Reynolds, impaled on that tree limb, how he emerged in the fog like a sailing ship figurehead, his mouth twisted and contorted from the pain.

Boggs realized he should've shot him then.

If he could've.

He thought of how fast Staunch went, completely obliterated by an enormous gob of venom. It had sounded like the most violent slap Boggs had ever heard, and then the sizzling and screams.

Boggs wondered how he'd survived. Just quick thinking, he guessed, and luck. It could've as easily been him as it was Staunch. Just pure, dumb shit luck.

Boggs crouched over in his chair, and cradled his head. He fought back his emotions as he thought of Staunch showing up at Sarah's funeral, laying a bouquet of roses down. He thought about how Staunch had hugged him in that cremation cemetery, and how Staunch had tears in his eyes at the time.

Everyone he knew that was good, had died.

Boggs stood and went over to Dagger's bunk room. He reached into the young soldier's clothing sack and retrieved a cigarette and lighter. Then he proceeded to open the ramp and walk down onto Mawholla.

The clouds had cleared overhead, revealing stars the likes of which Earth could not compete with. Light pollution now blanketed the continents on Earth. People could not see the night sky properly until they left Earth's orbit these days.

All sorts of things had gone wrong on Earth, the principle cause being overpopulation. Most of the coral reefs and oceans had died, the fisheries collapsed. The polar caps had melted, raising ocean levels and wiping out coastal cities. Summers now lasted most of the year, wiping out many crops. These brutally hot summers were only interrupted abruptly by disastrous winters that reached -50 degrees. It was appalling, really. One day it would be 110, and in two days everything would be frozen, only to lift again to 100 degrees a month later. The shoulder seasons were long gone, the gradual, subtle shifts of winter thawing into spring, and spring gently greening into summer. All of the keystone indicator species had gone, like grizzly bears, polar bears, the wolverine, lynx, and cold water species like trout. All of these species being present before meant the ecosystem was tremendously healthy. But overpopulation, sprawl, and climate change had other ideas. The national parks were killed off and developed, federal public land sold to the highest bidder (usually the oil companies). Once these important species and protections had vanished, humanity ran unchecked. Ghettos, starvation, disease, and poverty were the norms for 90% of Earth's citizens.

Before the last major collapse, CPB was formed, based on an initiative from the United Nations. All weapons and engineering manpower went to them, and a lottery was imposed on what remained of the human race...some 1 billion people.

Boggs took a drag on his cigarette, and watched as a shooting star lanced the sky.

The lucky lottery winners would get a trip to the first inhabitable planet. The catch?

Only 50,000 would be able to go.

Of course this caused mass, world-wide panic, with a violent uprising almost toppling CPB. But a targeted nuclear attack took care of the uprising's leaders, and the message was loud and clear.

Lottery winners were rounded up and kept in carefully guarded CPB fortresses.

And this was where Recon Elite came in. Recon, and the top engineers and biologists and their families wouldn't need a lottery. They were the first 1,000 to go. All of Boggs' training, and his men's was their Get-Out-Of-Jail free card.

Boggs wondered if he'd been crazy, trying to have a child with Sarah on such a fucked planet.

A twig snapped near the laser fence, and Boggs sprinted over to the noise with his dart gun.

The noise came again, near a group of mid-sized trees right at tree line.

Boggs relaxed when he realized it was the sleek squirrel-hunter. It looked at him with condescending eyes, and continued up into the canopy.

Boggs took another drag of his cigarette. It had been a long, long time since he'd smoked, and the nicotine made him buzz pleasantly.

The untracked wilderness of Mawholla pressed upon him as if a living, breathing entity. He felt all its weight, all its danger, all its beauty in one massive crush. For so long, humanity had their mother, Earth.

But apparently, they were all about to be born again.

25.

Boggs woke to someone tapping his shoulder.

Portman.

"You look like shit," Portman said to him, offering him a warm cup of coffee. "The machine just pissed this out."

Boggs cleared the night memories from his mind, to make room for the day. The coffee helped, and he got off his bunk, his leg muscles tight and cramping. Boggs grabbed a nutrient squeeze box from the refrigerator, then jabbed the plastic straw into it, and sucked.

After a few moments the cramping went away, thanks to a potent combination of potassium and magnesium. They'd been on the grind here, and endured considerable physical and psychological trauma. All of this was adding up, and they still had a long, long way to go.

Dagger appeared behind Portman, always with the nervous jitter in his eyes. But the kid was tough, Boggs would give him that. And sometimes toughness was all you needed to survive.

Boggs took another sip of coffee, and mentally got his shit together. "As soon as we suit up, we're going spitter hunting," he said, holding up the dart gun.

"Who's manning the Havoc 12?" Portman asked.

"You are," Boggs said.

"Can't wait to die today," Dagger said.

Boggs wanted to scold the kid, but his comment was kind of funny, with a hint of truth.

A few minutes later the men were geared up and rolling out. Dr. Tara and Dr. Volter were already in the yard, tinkering around with a small creature that had made it through the fence- or above it.

"It's a bird," Dr. Tara said. "A baby of some kind. I think it broke its wing."

Dr. Tara held a probe out to the bird. The tiny thing flapped its wings, and jabbed its beak at the probe.

"Feisty sucker," Dagger said. "Maybe we could have ourselves some chicken wings later."

"Oh please," Dr. Tara said, scooping up the bird and taking it into the CAV-121. "We have equipment to help it."

"Oh great," Dagger said. "I'm glad you have gear for birds."

Boggs shook his head. "Enough," he said to Dagger.

As Dr. Tara walked away, she glanced over her shoulder and smiled at Boggs.

Boggs smiled back, puffing his chest out a little as he did. That was all the encouragement he needed.

"Recon Elite," he said. "Are you ready to fuck up spitters?"

"Yes sir!" Dagger and Portman said in unison.

"Good," Boggs said. "Because that's exactly what we're going to do."

After creating a hole in the fence and sealing it, the men from Recon Elite entered Mawholla's wilderness.

Dr. Tara had given Boggs a new LifeForm meter, and it beeped away as squirrels, birds, and other neutral animals popped up on the screen.

Boggs stopped in the middle of the woods and adjusted the LifeForm settings so only animals over a certain mass appeared. If small poisonous animals crossed their path, the team might be in trouble. But that hadn't been the case so far, at least not in this rainforest environment.

The men hiked deep into the forest, saying nothing, intent and focused on their mission. Soon they reached the ravine where they'd found Dr. Reynolds' shirt. The huge log, and several others crossed the gorge, creating a God-like stair step that disappeared into dense fog.

Boggs turned to his men, his breath visible as he exhaled.

"We're going to cross that log," he said. "And that's important because this ravine acts as a territorial boundary between the spitters and another species." Boggs pointed to markings on either side of the gorge wall...one side clearly the venom from the spitters, and the other a reddish hue that the men hadn't seen before.

"That's territorial behavior marking," Boggs said, pointing at both spots. "Are you locked and loaded?" Boggs said to his men above the misty gorge.

"Yes sir," the men whispered.

"Good," Boggs said. "Because today, the fate of mankind rests in our hands. We are the tip of the spear. I cannot emphasize that enough. We are the first hope. We are Lewis and Clark. Hell, fellas, we're bigger than Lewis and Clark."

"Who's Lewis and Clark?" Dagger asked.

"Jesus Christ," Portman said. "Are you kidding me?"

Boggs turned to Dagger in the fog as numerous insects called out from the tree canopy across the gorge. "Lewis and Clark were great explorers," Boggs said. "Legendary."

"Okay," Dagger said. "So you're saying we're great explorers."

Boggs grinned at Dagger. "The greatest," he said.

The men used the giant fallen log to cross the ravine. A hush fell over the land, and only the footfalls of the men were heard.

Boggs pointed northwest, to where he and Staunch had been ambushed. Soon the limb where Dr. Reynolds had been impaled appeared in the mist. The only trace of his existence was the deep crimson stain covering half the limb.

"That it?" Dagger asked.

Boggs nodded.

"Where the hell did he go?" Dagger asked.

"They probably ate him," Portman said.

Dagger winced. "Fuckin thing. Fucking cannibal things."

"You'll get your chance to get at 'em," Boggs said. "Just stay patient. We're going to need a better plan."

Dagger looked incredulous. "You mean you don't have one?"

"There is indeed a plan," Boggs said. "But I'm going to add to it. Come on, get your frag nades counted. We're going to need them."

26.

As they moved further north and higher into the mountains, Boggs' lungs burned as oxygen became more fleeting. He popped an aspirin to alleviate the tightness, something he was doing more of these days.

What remained of Recon Elite was up in rugged country now, big jumbles of rocks and downed trees. Boggs felt tiny in all this...no, *was* tiny. They passed crevasses, some of them containing mid-sized animals the LifeForm meter considered neutral. The shapes on the screen looked cat-like, which made sense to Boggs, because they never saw one of the things with their own eyes. And back home on Earth, wild cats were known to steer clear of trouble, rather than confront it. A single injury to a wildcat meant death. They needed their dexterity to be able to catch prey. Without it, they were fucked.

"Damn things spook me out," Dagger said. "Wish they'd come out."

"No you don't" Boggs said.

Boggs checked the muddy trail. In it, he saw footprints of a spitter. Dr. Tara had told him the spitters likely lived at a higher elevation, coming down from rocky slopes and alpine cirques. Something about their claws and physical makeup had made her come to that conclusion.

She'd also said something about prey, and rearing habitat. Dr. Tara inferred they'd likely shelter their young in higher life zones, and then travel in packs to the lower elevation woodlands to hunt.

Boggs and his men had been the hunted.

But no more. Now it was time to go on offense. Just like the NFL playoffs, or political campaigns, prevent defense was a recipe for failure. A strong team, a strong candidate keeps up the attack on their opponent until the contest has been decided.

Boggs thought back to his history books, and how the monstrous German army had been defeated in World War II. They'd had a remarkable string of successes, buoyed by a new kind of fighting style called the "blitzkrieg". They'd taken many countries with this method, and then attacked Russia with the same tactic, capturing massive territories. Where the Germans went wrong however, was splitting apart a group that was headed for Moscow, postponing the main attack by weeks. This was the opposite of what the Germans had done before.

There'd been two World Wars since then on Earth, one in 2020, another in 2112. Millions had been lost, and tactical nukes had been deployed in places like North Korea and China. But humans still couldn't match the 60 million death toll in World War II. Something about being slapped with a tactical nuke made everyone calm the fuck down.

And maybe, that was exactly what the spitters needed. Not a tactical nuke, but a Havoc 12, set to multi-fire mode right in the middle of their rearing habitat.

Boggs understood the importance of sending a message. This was also learned, initially, from his study of history. Near the end of World War II, the Japanese had refused to surrender. So the U.S. sent a message in the form of an atom bomb. Japan still did not quite grasp that message, and an atom bomb was dropped again. After that, the Japanese surrendered.

And that was the goal with the spitters. Send a powerful enough message to leave humans the fuck alone. Let the DNA virus kill off one third of the population (as Dr. Tara estimated), and let the Havoc send the other message. And if obeyed, the two species could co-exist, potentially. If not, they were on the list to be wiped out. Doctor's orders.

After what they'd done to his men, Boggs was okay with the latter. More than okay, in fact.

The men climbed higher and higher, at last breaking through the fog. The view left Boggs speechless. For hundreds of miles in every direction loomed snowcapped peaks, cloaked in thick clouds, which carpeted the ancient valley forests from where they'd just come.

"Holy shit," Dagger said. "Aint never seen anything like this."

Far down in the valley, the eagle they'd seen the day before soared just above the clouds, then dove into them at full speed, wings tucked tight like a missile.

The two suns beamed off embedded glaciers in the highest peaks far above them. Boggs heard a terrible rumbling, and pulled out his binoculars and watched as a snow field crashed down a far off mountain, causing huge chunks of ice to crack free, like breaking bones on an enormous creature. A powerful wind roared across the mountains, bending the scrawny trees mercilessly. In a meadow perhaps a thousand feet above, a herd of the moose-like animals grazed, looking down at Recon Elite every so often.

"Where the fuck do the spitters live?" Dagger asked as he lit up one of his cigarettes.

Boggs gestured to the ground, about five feet in front of Dagger. "Open your eyes," he said. "Classic spitter track."

"Fuck," Dagger said. "Sorry sir."

"Don't apologize for things you don't need to apologize for," Boggs said. "I know you're alert. But be smart alert, too."

Boggs set the dart gun down and glassed the high meadows with his binoculars. Above the herd of moose-like animals, the meadow turned into rock scree, and then met a cliff wall that towered thousands of feet. But what caught Boggs' eye the most was the numerous high cave entrances that penetrated the cliff at its base.

Portman stole Dagger's cigarette, and took a drag. "So the spitters come out of the caves there, like the Grinch, and sneak up on us, and other animals," he said.

"That's exactly what they do," Boggs said. "And did you notice anything else, Recon Elite?"

Dagger looked down at his feet and bit his lip. "They seem to be mostly night creatures," he said.

"That's right," Boggs said. "Nocturnal, mostly. Which is why the heavy fog yesterday worked to their advantage."

An abrasive clicking and hissing sound came from down in the valley, beneath the layer of clouds. Boggs turned and headed for a cluster of rocks that almost reminded him of the rock statues at Easter Island.

Once inside the rocks, Boggs peered out of an opening.

The sound turned out to be what he thought it was, a congregation of the pig-crabs, clacking their way up the rocks past the wind-busted trees.

The moose creatures that had been feeding in the high meadow bolted to the west, downslope and out of view. The crab-pigs moved at outrageous speeds, which blew Boggs' mind. Soon the creatures were up in the meadow, scooping up feces with their limbs and tossing it onto their backs, then rolling around on the grass.

Boggs heard a roar come from the cliff base, just above the high meadow. He raised his binoculars and watched as a spitter glared back at the crabs.

The pack of crabs stopped what they were doing, and stood on hind legs, their mouths snapping shut, then gaping, then snapping shut.

"Holy shit," Dagger said. "Looks like we got us a Mawholla bastard stand-off."

But Boggs knew better. The spitters were too clever, and most likely wouldn't tolerate this intrusion into their territory, daylight or not.

The first spitter that emerged from the cave looked irritated as hell, its eyes narrow slits, and kicking up rock spree and dust as it ran. But oddly (at least to Boggs), the spitter ran right towards the crabs, and stopped halfway.

Uh-oh, Boggs thought. The crabs were fucked. And since they were fucked, he wanted a name for them.

"Crigs," Boggs said to Dagger.

"Speak English please, sir," Dagger said.

"That's their name. 'Crigs'."

"Whatever you say sir," Dagger said.

The crigs squealed with delight at the spitter's apparent stupid behavior, and hurried their way towards it. The spitter stood right where it was.

When the crigs reached two-thirds of the way to the spitter, the spitter turned and glanced back to a higher cave.

A big momma thundered from the cave entrance, already at full speed, head low to the ground, feet kicking up high behind it.

The crigs hissed and tried to flee, but the big momma was on them, pouncing with her vast jaws and rending the crigs as if they were nothing.

Just brutal, Boggs thought. He had great dislike for both species, but watching a massacre was never easy. Ever.

The crigs, although able to spit venom, simply weren't as good at it as the spitters. Their velocity and reach was no match.

What the big momma couldn't finish by sheer force, the smaller spitter took care of with its venom. Soon another spitter joined, and then one more. As big momma crushed and maimed the helpless crigs, the smaller spitters delivered carefully aimed sprays to crigs' mouths and heads, then cleanly severed the heads and left them to rot.

In a matter of seconds, it was over.

The upper meadow lay slick with glistening blood as sunlight baked the mess.

The spitters dragged the headless crigs back to the caves, no doubt for dinner time.

"Fucking sick," Dagger said.

"It's nature up this way," Portman said. "We're in store for a lot of this."

Boggs had thought he'd seen it all. But the absolute deviousness of the spitters was starting to make itself clearer and clearer. The trap with Dr. Reynolds had been bad enough, but the way they baited an entire herd of crigs had been especially devious.

Boggs made sure Portman still had the Havoc 12.

He did. Boggs knew he did.

But as he turned, Boggs saw something else. A brief outline of an animal that was there, and then suddenly gone.

Boggs rubbed his dry eyes, and refocused where the blanket of clouds met the mountain slopes to the south. The figure was a familiar one, almost mocking, the way it yapped its wolf-like jaws.

Had he just seen Jekyll?

Impossible, Boggs thought. Jekyll lived hundreds of miles to the north.

Or was it?

He thought of asking Dagger and Portman if they'd seen anything back downslope, at the edge of the clouds. But he could tell they hadn't seen a thing by the looks on their faces.

Boggs closed his eyes and took a deep breath, then sipped from his nutrient straw. He wondered if the pressure of exploring Mawholla was starting to take its toll on him.

Jekyll, he thought. *You crafty son of a bitch.*

He pictured the northern tundra, and the far off rise of Pine Tree Ridge, and the way Jekyll half-trotted to the horizon.

"Sir, I think I see something coming," Dagger said from his side of the rock pile.

"Jekyll?" Boggs asked.

Dagger furrowed his brow. "Uh no," he said. "Not even close."

Dagger pointed upslope. A spitter emerged from a cave entrance, carrying a picked-clean carcass from a headless crig. It dragged the carcass to a point further along the cliff wall, then disappeared.

"Hate those things," Dagger said.

"Tell me something I don't know," Boggs said.

"Okay," Dagger said, gripping his ZR-15 nervously. "Since you asked, I thought I saw something last night."

"Go on," Boggs said, careful to keep his voice down.

"I went out to have a smoke, late. Real late. More like early morning. I walked over to the fence, and saw a flash of something about twenty feet back in the dark. It was staring at me, kinda mocking me, you know?"

"What was it?" Boggs asked.

"I think it was Jekyll. But I can't say for sure, sir."

Goosebumps coursed up Boggs' limbs. He turned to Portman.

"What about you?"

Portman shook his head. "I've seen a couple things flash out of the corner of my eye, but I can't say for sure."

"But was it fast?" Boggs asked.

"Yes. Almost too fast to be real."

Boggs was stunned. Was it all a coincidence?

"How the fuck could it be Jekyll?" Dagger asked.

"Anything's possible," Boggs said, not sure if he believed it himself. "Jekyll is blink-of-an-eye fast. He could theoretically speed down here. But I doubt he can move like that for very long."

"What the fuck does he want with us?" Dagger asked.

Boggs shrugged. "Don't know. He's sneaky."

"Hell yeah he is," Dagger said as he turned his attention to the north, and up the mountain. "The spitter is back, and no carcass this time."

Boggs inched forward and looked. Sure enough, the spitter returned to its cave without the carcass.

"Must have taken it to a disposal area," Boggs said. An idea flashed in his mind that electrified him.

Boggs huddled with the last of Recon Elite. "We can't face them head on," he said. "We need to bait one of them, like they baited us."

"Oh hell yeah," Dagger said.

26.

The men hiked their way around the upper meadow where the slaughter had taken place, careful to hug the western slope, just out of view of the spitter caves. They were able to reach the base of a horn prominence, which had blocked their view of what the spitter had done with the crig's carcass. From there they hiked west, then northeast around the horn until at last they dropped down into a gulley that bordered the massive cliffs, and thus the spitter caves. Boggs and his men worked down a stair step-like series of mountain rock, careful not to slip on a thin ribbon of waterfall that must've dropped thousands of feet from the peaks to the north.

When they finished climbing down the rocks, Boggs was shocked at what he saw. The men arrived at a pit of sorts, clearly dug out by the spitters themselves, almost like a rock quarry back on Earth. The pit was home to an immeasurable number of bones, rotting meat, and other disturbing sights. Flies the size of tennis balls buzzed and wiggled out of eye sockets in oversized skulls, their tubular larva squirming in the ribcages. Something unseen slithered beneath the bones, and then another.

"Do not step in there at the moment," Boggs said.

Instead, the men made their way around the western flank.

The smell was nauseating.

A pair of tennis ball-sized flies wiggled out of a dead crig's ribcage, and buzzed inches from Dagger's face. Dagger unsheathed his survival knife and sliced off a wing in mid-air, sending the fly spinning in a mad circle until it buzzed and flopped in a pile of bones.

"Good work," Boggs said. "A hunter never takes a shot unless he knows it's a kill shot."

The maimed fly beat its half wing faster and faster, and then died.

"See, I killed it," Dagger said.

Boggs made firm eye contact with him. "You don't kill a thing unless I say you can. Got it?"

"Yes sir."

Boggs pried loose a bone from a crig carcass and heaved it into a section of the pit closest to where the spitter caves had been. Something slithered under the bones, away from where the bone had been tossed.

Boggs climbed down into the carcasses, and waved for his men to join him.

"You sick fuck," Portman said with a grin. "But I like your style."

"God Damnit," Dagger said as he waded in. "Just...just god Damnit."

A minute later they sat amongst the bones. Boggs used hunks of rotting carcasses to partially conceal himself. But he kept the dart gun barrel exposed and aimed at the pit's lip, closest to the spitter dens, which were out of sight from their lowered pit vantage point. But Boggs knew there were many more headless crig carcasses back in those caves, and sooner or later, another carcass would be dragged out.

The men sat there amidst the chunky flies and waited.

And waited.

The two suns sunk behind the mountains, and occasionally a slithering sound wound its way towards them, which Boggs warded off with a rattle of bones.

At dusk, a form appeared from the south and headed towards the lip.

It was a spitter, covered in crig blood and gripping a carcass in its claws. The insatiated spitter's belly bulged, and it moved groggily as it approached the pit.

The engorged spitter bit into the carcass, then heaved it into the pit, sending up rotting tendrils of flesh and scattering bones. A stench belched forth as the bones were disrupted, and Dagger gagged.

The spitter hissed, and stared straight into the area where Boggs and his men were hidden.

Boggs pulled the trigger.

The dart flew through the air at a rate of speed Boggs would describe as 'pathetic'. But before the spitter could dodge, the dart found its mark in its soft neck tissue. The spitter hissed and roared, then pulled out the dart with its mouth. It looked back in the direction the dart came from, then towards the cave, and let out what could only be considered an alarm cry.

"Holy shit," Dagger said. "We're fucked."

Then the spitter did exactly what Boggs hoped it would do: it raced to meet the others it had alerted.

Boggs flicked his finger, making sure Dagger had seen it. "Aim ahead of it," Boggs said. "To scare the others from the pit."

Dagger chucked a frag nade high into the air, and it exploded twelve feet above the ground ahead of the original spitter. The once-darted spitter roared again and sprinted at the men, as a big momma and two satellite spitters thundered up the canyon towards the pit.

"Fuck me," Portman said.

Boggs and Dagger hurled two frag nades, exploding them at ten feet, and thirty feet respectively.

The remaining members of Recon Elite scrambled out of the carcass pit, then sprinted along the eastern edge and up the rocks from where they'd entered.

But it wasn't enough, of course. By the time they'd gotten one third of the way up, the spitters were crashing through the pit, sending bones and rotting sinew flying in all directions.

Boggs turned to look. To his horror, all four spitters stopped at the base of the rocks, and reared back to launch their deadly venom.

"Oh shit," Dagger said.

He and Boggs flung down two nades. Upon exploding, rock shrapnel shot into the spitters' eyes, enraging them.

"Don't nade the darted spitter," Boggs said. "We need it to stay alive and infect the others."

"I can't help what I kill right now," Dagger screamed.

"I agree," Portman said, his back to the steep rocks, the Havoc 12 aimed and ready.

Undeterred, the spitters readied to spit again.

"Fire the Havoc 12," Boggs said.

Portman pressed the trigger and the LCD screen lit up. Its computer instantly recognized the spitter's composition, and it locked target accordingly. The bullet flew out of the launch tube, then rocketed down the slope and straight into the enormous eye of a big momma.

Boggs heard a grotesque squishing sound as the big momma roared and pawed at its damaged eye.

But the Havoc 12 wasn't done. The bullet was milling around in the big momma's skull. And when the great beast collapsed into the carcass pit, Boggs had figured the bullet finally found its brain, or its brain stem.

The bullet exited out the back of the big momma's head just as a half dozen spitters hurtled towards the carcass pit.

"Go," Boggs said. "Climb like the devils I know you are."

He and his men did just that as the Havoc 12 bullet did its job below them. Boggs could hear the crunching of gristle and bone, the tearing of flesh and the horrible cries from the dying spitters.

And as far as he could tell, none of their venom had reached his men. And he was incredibly proud about that.

"Climb you motherfuckers climb," Boggs said. "Or I'll have you doing pushups back at camp. Is that clear?"

"Yes sir!" his men said.

As Boggs climbed, he admired their determination to complete the mission, and to survive on top of it.

Boggs gazed far below. Five dead or dying spitters lay contorted in the carcass pit. But a big momma had caught the Havoc 12 bullet as it was slowing down to a right angle, and knocked it against a cliff wall. The alpine cirque filled with a tremendous bang, and then settled into an ominous quiet as the big momma began to climb, too.

"What the fuck was that?" Dagger said, not yet looking below.

"Don't look," Boggs said. "Keep climbing."

But Boggs looked. The big momma was moving fast…too fast for his liking.

Above the men, the steep rock segued into a smoother grassy pitch, and then wrapped around the horn back downhill to where they'd come from.

But Boggs knew they'd never outrun a big momma in open terrain, or by even climbing. If not for the head start and diversion caused by the Havoc 12, they'd all be dead already.

The men reached the grassy slope, and sprinted around the horn as fast as they could muster without breaking bones. When Boggs looked back, the big momma had reached the lip of the rocks, and glared at the men hungrily.

"Sir," Portman said. "May I fire another Havoc 12?"

"Fire away," Boggs said.

Portman took a knee, then fired the Havoc 12. The bullet rocketed out of the tube, but instead of slowing down and adjusting for the big momma, it flew straight and true into the afternoon sky, and exploded against the far cliffs.

"Frag nades," Boggs said.

The men heaved three at once, which exploded within feet of the charging big momma's eyes. She stumbled into the base of the horn, and Boggs wondered if they'd blinded her.

"More," Boggs said.

The men hurled three more frag nades, again exploding at the big momma's head level.

The enormous creature roared in pain, then clawed at her eyes.

Boggs fired his ZR-15 into the soft underbelly, listening to the bullets make wet, meaty sounds as they penetrated skin.

Dagger and Portman followed, and soon the big momma was clutching her abdomen, then teetering into the base of the horn.

The men did not relent.

A moment later it was over, the big momma taking her last breath, and lying still.

"Holy smokes," Dagger said. "That's our first big momma kill."

"Come on," Boggs said. "The others will be here soon, if they're not on their way already."

The last of Recon Elite hiked around the horn, then dropped down into the high meadow, and back into the first layer of clouds they'd emerged from earlier. Before being entirely swallowed, Boggs looked back up the slope towards the spitter caves. The foreground before the caves was teeming with movement, and Boggs realized it was a swarm of spitters, all charging towards himself, Portman and Dagger.

And boy did they look pissed off.

27.

There was no time to outrun the spitters. Boggs and his men reached the ravine with the gigantic fallen log, and decided to climb down the cliff face, far enough so they were obscured by the fog closer to the unseen river.

All three men had been trained to climb, and descend. It was part of their PET, or "planet expeditionary training". They'd left their packs hidden amongst rocks and ferns, along with the Havoc 12.

The cliff walls were cold and slimy, providing poor purchase for both toes and fingers alike. But once in a while Boggs found a sheltered cranny that was not moist. Soon, all three men lowered themselves into the gorge fog, the sound of the river rushing far below them. Boggs looked up at the weak filtered suns, and the outline of the ancient log running from edge to edge. Portman clung to Boggs' right, and Dagger to his left, but down a few feet.

Dagger looked up at Boggs, his eyes wide and jittery.

"This is some stupid shit, sir," Dagger said. "Worse than that shitty worm tunnel you took us down. Worse than all of it."

Portman spat a gob of phlegm down into the river, as if an answer to Dagger's complaints.

"Careful, Dr. Tara wouldn't like you introducing invasive bacteria to the ecosystem," Dagger said as he smirked.

Boggs adjusted his grip, and dropped down another ten feet. "There's a good-sized ledge down another twenty," he said. "Can you two make it? I don't want to hang here all day."

"Think so," Dagger said as he edged his way to the right. As he did, a small pile of rocks shucked loose and tumbled into the ravine's maw.

Portman started working his way over too, just as a shadow rose out of the fog and towards the men.

And no one could do a damn thing until they reached the ledge.

"It's the eagle," Dagger said.

The eagle swooped by the men, way too close, then circled back for another look.

"It's trying to knock us off," Portman said. "So it can eat us along the riverbed."

The eagle emerged from the fog again, in a slight variation of its previous pattern. The bird was eerily casual in its movement.

Since Portman was first in its path, he held his arm out and tried to swat it, but it was a feeble attempt. Instead he almost lost his footing.

The eagle buzzed Dagger, and then disappeared into the ravine below.

"Fuckin' thing," Dagger said. "Just toying with us for its own amusement."

Boggs had noticed the creatures of Mawholla seemed to have a knack for that. He wondered what had caused them to behave that way along their evolutionary path. A deadly planet, but also a planet of pranksters…at least so far from what they'd seen.

The men finally reached the ledge, just wide enough for all three to crouch safely, ZR-15s aimed and ready if need be.

Boggs thought he glimpsed movement above, along the dim outline of the fallen log.

Spitters.

The creatures ran along the length of the log from ravine edge to ravine edge, a train of them, their unique tails snaking over the side, or curling slightly-off center above the log's outline. Boggs watched for a minute, and at last the final spitter crossed the log, its tail curling in anticipation of the hunt.

Dagger watched, too, and even he didn't say a peep. Doing so would've been certain death, with the spitters lobbing down copious amounts of venom at a static target, with gravity as their friend.

Boggs waited five minutes.

Finally, Dagger spoke: "They're going to attack Base Camp," he said.

Boggs shook his head. "They won't attack it straight on. They're hatching a plan. Or already have one."

"So," Dagger said. "That just means we need a better one."

Boggs turned to Portman. "What the hell happened with that last Havoc shot?" he whispered.

"Dunno," Portman said. "Thing just failed to lock on."

"CPB engineers had indicated a small failure rate, both on initial accuracy, and in terms of unintended targeting. We got the short straw, unfortunately."

"I have two more bullets in my bag," Portman said. "I just haven't had time to load them yet."

"Good," Boggs said. "We're going to need them. The spitters are probably laying a trap right now, with the intent of taking down the fence, and taking out the CAVs as well. Our job will be to distract them from that mission."

Dagger lit up a cigarette, cupping the sparking lighter with his fingers. "What about the DNA virus?" he asked. "What's the effect on that?"

Boggs sighed. The truth was ugly, and he hated giving it. "Look at how many of them just crossed the log," he said. "I don't think it's had much of an effect. At this point it's especially difficult to say."

Dagger took a drag, and frowned. "So all that was a total waste of time. And on top of it, we stirred the shit out of them."

Boggs felt a flash of anger, and let it fade before speaking. "We did what we were ordered to do by CPB biologists," he said. "We are the spearhead, and we carry out missions crucial to the survival of the human race. Do you have a problem with that, Dagger? Do you have a problem with saving the human race?"

"No sir," Dagger said.

"Good," Boggs said. "Now put that god damn cigarette out before you give us away with the scent."

"Yes sir," Dagger said as he pinched off the tobacco and crushed it under his boot.

Silence fell between the men, the weight of an entire wilderness planet. Below, the river pounded against rocks, out of sight, but Boggs heard the powerful current gouging out huge pools. He wondered what kind of fish lived in those pools, and what color the water was.

They had only been on Mawholla so long, and lost so much already. He would do everything within his power to prevent another death from the spearhead. Recon Elite or biologists.

Boggs knew what he had to do next. He'd give it another fifteen minutes, then crawl through the forest, placing Recon Elite behind the first line of spitters. From there he and his men would observe their gait and health, to see if the DNA virus had begun to work...or not work. Once that step was complete, he'd fire the Havoc 12 himself. It wasn't that he didn't trust Portman, he just wanted to see what went wrong with the Havoc, if anything did. This way he could report back to CPB why the Havoc 12 was malfunctioning.

Far below, the unseen river gouged out pools, the way humans had gouged out almost all the viable natural resources from mother Earth.

And here they were again.

"Man, we're really in this mess aren't we?" Portman asked Boggs as they huddled on the ledge.

"We're alright," Boggs said.

"Never been better," Dagger said. "Jesus man."

It had been a good while since the bulk of the spitters passed, so Boggs caved and let the men share a cigarette. He enjoyed the camaraderie despite circumstances. And that was the thing. On this job, and back on Earth, circumstances were always shitty. A man had to find bright spots even when things looked bleak. Even Boggs took a drag or two, just to show he was one of the guys.

"You and Dr. Tara," Dagger said, "You two seem to like each other a lot."

"Anything is possible," Boggs said. "But you never know. We've only had a few dates. Sometimes you can tell from a few dates, sometimes you can't."

Boggs took a drag off his cigarette. "A man has to play it cool early. We fall in love way too fast. Women are more about slow and steady."

Dagger nodded. "Do you think we've let enough of the spitters pass yet?"

"No," Boggs said. "Pack animals such as the spitters will have one or two trails that follow far behind the pack to make sure they're not being ambushed. If we go out too soon, we'll trip up their defenses. We want them at the laser fence, bunched up so the Havoc 12 can do the most damage.

Boggs' COMM device beeped.

"Shit," Portman said. "That thing is going to give us away."

It was Dr. Tara.

Boggs faced the ledge, to muffle his talking.

"Sam," she said. "Numerous spitters have appeared twenty yards out from the fence in all directions."

"Are they doing anything, or just watching?" Boggs asked.

"Watching," Dr. Tara said. "But some are looking behind them, as if waiting for something."

"They're waiting for tailers," Boggs said.

"Are you safe?" Dr. Tara asked.

"Yes, for now," Boggs asked. "We're going to hit them from behind with the Havoc. Be aware of crossfire if you decide to use the external canons. We're going to be fifty to seventy yards north from the fence."

"Got it, Sam," Dr. Tara said. "And I know this is totally unprofessional, but I hope we get another date soon."

Boggs chuckled. "Yeah, I know a great pizza place just round the corner."

Dr. Tara laughed. "Sam, you always had a way with words. Be safe, and I'll see you soon."

"Back at you," Boggs said as he switched his COMM device into silent mode.

Portman shook his head. "Man are you whipped," he said.

28.

Once Boggs and his men hiked down the rocky terrain and reached the valley floor, they crawled. This tactic provided excellent cover beneath the ferns. Boggs held his LifeForm meter out in front of him, as his elbows dug into the spongy forest floor. The meter picked up creatures seventy yards ahead in the woods.

"There the fuckers are," Dagger whispered to Boggs.

Boggs put a finger to his pursed lips, then crawled forward. Soon the men reached a tiny ridge that offered an excellent viewpoint of the forest. The two suns filtered through the canopy in random spots, illuminating what appeared to be a great hall of sorts, the trees like ancient pillars. And at the far end of the spectacle, a dozen spitters milled about, some of them pacing, some sitting perfectly still, eyes towards the laser fence.

"How many do you think there are, total?" Dagger asked.

"Probably the same amount on every side of the fence," Boggs said, doing his best to hide his concern for Dr. Tara. "They aren't messing around this time. They might all charge."

Portman chuckled. "They'll get sliced to bits," he said. "I hope they do."

"That would be too easy," Dagger said. "That wouldn't fit with everything that's happened since we've been here."

"That's going to change," Boggs said. "We're going to change it today. Right here, right now. Good luck is not about happenstance, it's created through hard work. And we're working our asses off today."

Boggs studied the spitters, looking for signs of sickness. But the entire herd on this side of the fence looked perfectly healthy. *Not cool,* he thought.

He wanted something, any kind of weakness or "in".

As they waited in the old growth forest, in this hall of giants, Boggs wondered about the Havoc 12. Would it misfire again? Revealing their position and causing certain death?

Boggs got to his knees and aimed the tube, half pressing the trigger and initiating a LifeForm lock sequence.

A few seconds later, the LCD readout indicated the Havoc had achieved target lock on the spitters. But that was an awful long time for a Havoc 12 to respond. Boggs wondered if the humidity was starting to negatively affect the equipment. It was possible. Hell, anything was possible on Mawholla.

Boggs turned to his men. "You ready, Recon Elite?"

"Yes sir," Dagger and Portman said in unison.

Boggs squeezed the Havoc 12 trigger. The bullet rocketed from the tube and streaked across the great hall of giant trees like an errant sparkler.

As it flew, half the spitters looked back. But it wasn't the bullet they'd noticed at first, but rather the THWUMP sound the bullet made as it left the tube. A major flaw, obviously. Boggs made a mental note for Dr. Tara, and CPB engineers.

Before the first spitter could dodge, the bullet entered its chest, and plowed through guts and gristle until it exited out the spitter's lower spine area, then cutting a hard angle and accelerating before burrowing into the head of a heftier spitter, but not quite the size of a big momma.

Boggs watched the madness unfold with a sense of pride. He no longer felt any sort of guilt over killing a native species…especially not after what the spitters did to Dr. Reynolds. It was almost as if the spitters knew they were doing the wrong thing.

The spitters on the north side of the fence scurried about, snapping and swiping at the bullet as it slowed, accelerated, and slowed again. Their tails whipped wildly in the air, chopping up ferns and lower branches.

Yet the Havoc 12 bullet continued on its path of destruction, blowing out a spitter at the knees, as it screamed and clawed the air.

Dagger clenched his ZR-15, and watched with wild eyes. "How many can it kill before the bullet wears down?" he asked.

"CPB engineers estimated up to five hundred targets of standard biological composition. But the spitters are not your standard biological composition. The bullet is coming into contact with their corrosive venom, which is probably going to wear down the components," Boggs said.

"Jesus," Dagger said. "So how many you think?"

"Maybe fifty spitters," Boggs said.

Boggs turned his attention back to the forest cathedral and the violence at the far end. The spitters still hadn't caught onto where the bullet had come from, but they *were* dispersing to the east and west. A few foolish spitters remained, and were annihilated by the bullet, one in the brain, one in the gut and through the rectum, one through the knee.

After killing the last few spitters on the north side, the Havoc 12 bullet accelerated after the herd that had branched off to the west.

"Come on," Boggs said. "This is our chance."

The men raced through the forest cathedral, keeping their heads as low as possible. Soon they arrived at the scene of the massacre, and had to weave their way around bone fragments, paralyzed spitters, and gobs of blood and entrails. When they reached the laser fence Boggs created a small hole with the Little Beaver, and continued towards CAV-121.

The ramp opened at once, and next Boggs found himself in the main cabin. Dr. Tara approached him, looking worried.

"Did it work?" she asked.

"No time," Boggs said. "We need to get out of here. Set your coordinates for the usual spot in the tundra zone."

"The laser fence can handle the spitters," Dr. Tara said.

"Not this time," Boggs said. "Things have changed. They're bringing the cavalry, and the Havoc 12 could only take out a dozen or so."

Boggs turned to Portman. "Stay here," he said. "Dagger, you're coming with me."

Dagger followed Boggs out of the CAV-121, and into the 117.

"Danni," Boggs said. "Take us back north to the tundra location."

"Yes Captain," Danni said.

As the engines fired up, Boggs turned to the console monitors. The spitters that had been twenty to thirty yards outside the laser fence now stood right next to it.

Most of them were big mommas.

Boggs observed smaller spitters racing through the woods, then along the backs of the big mommas, using them as ramps to hurtle over the top of the laser fencing.

"Holy shit," Dagger said.

Boggs reached for his COMM device. "Dr. Tara, fire up your CAV NOW!"

"We are," Dr. Tara said. "Spitters have breached the fencing."

Boggs switched the camera view to the CAV's rear, and watched in horror as numerous spitters clung to CAV-121. To his utter shock, several of them were running full throttle into the CAV's engines, mucking up the turbines and propulsion systems.

"Sam," Dr. Tara said through her COMM. "We're taking damage."

In the madness, Boggs watched as the CAV-121 bay door opened and Portman ran outside. He fired wildly at the spitters that slammed into the engines. Boggs seized control of the external canons and fired again and again at the onslaught. A big momma ran up the back of a fence-side spitter and leapt over the top, crashing down into Base Camp 1.

A second later the big momma was on top of CAV-121, ripping out shielding and wires.

Portman dropped to one knee and fired off the Havoc 12, penetrating the rampaging big momma through her left eye.

Boggs slammed the ramp button, and raced outside with his ZR-15, Dagger on his heels.

The men couldn't fire without damaging the ship, but it was crawling with spitters. Boggs watched in utter dismay as Portman became inundated with their venom. He screamed and clutched his melting face, then collapsed to the ground.

Numb with shock, Boggs raced back up inside the CAV-117 with Dagger, then closed the ramp. He took over manual controls, and hovered fifty feet above CAV-121.

Dr. Tara screamed on the COMM.

"They have us," she said. "Sam please help us."

Even more spitters leapt over the fencing, some of their tails getting sliced off as they hung low during the jump. The tailless, blood-spurting spitters gummed up the engines as they kamikazeed into them.

As CAV-117 hovered over the damaged CAV-121, Boggs had a decision to make. He could risk permanently damaging 121 by firing upon the swarming spitters, or he could let them take the ship.

It was then he realized there was no choice at all.

He fired the external canons, immolating spitter after spitter, and racking up heavy damage to CAV-121. These ships had never been designed for space battle, because there had never been any proof of an advanced alien civilization. They were designed to fend off hostile, less intelligent creatures.

The spitters had proved more than a match.

Countless spitters leapt the fence now, and Boggs wondered if their entire cave population at higher elevation hadn't completely emptied.

He continued to fire as Dagger stood at his side and said nothing, mouth agape.

Sparks and blood and bits of bone filled the sky in a grotesque mist.

And for a while, it looked like he was winning.

But a peculiar thing caught Boggs' attention…a thing that shouldn't have happened at all. A careless, god damn foolish deadly thing. Someone inside had failed to close the ramp bay after Portman had left.

Boggs watched as two spitters snuck up the ramp. Then he heard the screams on his COMM device.

"Close the ramp!" Boggs yelled into the COMM. "Close the ramp, close the ramp, close the ramp!"

But no one answered, save for the voice of Dr. Volter, which was making surreal, guttural noises that Boggs could not stand to listen to.

Yet he kept his COMM on, and kept firing, picking off the remaining spitters until no more clung to the battered and bloodied CAV-121. Then Boggs turned to the big mommas that had made it possible to jump the fence. He unloaded on them, again and again, until they retreated into the forest with knowing, devious eyes.

Boggs lowered the CAV to twenty feet over the 121. Two spitters emerged down the ramp, carrying the headless bodies of Dr. Tara and Dr. Volter.

Boggs fired on them, imploding their skulls in red mist explosions. Next he ran a LifeForm sweep of Base Camp 1, and then landed the CAV-117.

"Jesus Christ," Dagger said. "Sweet lord almighty, what have we done?"

Boggs opened the ramp, and ran over to Dr. Tara and Dr. Volter's bodies. They had not been spit on, there was no need to. The spitters had done their dirty work up close. The last two members of Recon Elite carried the bodies up into the CAV-117. As Dagger took the bodies, Boggs hurried over to the 121, and placed the severed heads of Dr. Volter and the beautiful woman he had grown so fond of into a biological bag. Then he used a remote device he grabbed from the console to close CAV-121's ramp.

He said nothing to Dagger. But he did say things to himself. He cursed himself, cursed this mission, and cursed God, if there ever was such a thing. Cursed all creation as the weight of severed heads tugged at his right arm.

"Danni," Boggs said back inside CAV-117. "Take us to the coordinates in the tundra," he said.

Then Boggs began the work of zipping up the remains, and storing them in the ship's rear compartment.

What have we done, Boggs thought. *Dear God, what are we doing, and what are we going to do?*

29.

Boggs had Danni land the ship near the worm tunnel breach he and Dagger had created during their escape.

It was dark now, and Boggs sat in his console chair, numb as a chunk of ice. He listened to the ship whine down around him. The CAV-117 vents sucked in the pure Mawholla air, cooling the cabin after a filtration process.

Dagger sat behind Boggs, his head in his hands.

"We've never gotten sick," Dagger said. "It's weird. You think we'd have caught something weird by now."

Boggs didn't want to speak, hell, didn't want to live. But he was a man, and a leader. And he still had a job to do.

"You know that tetanus shot they gave us before we left port?" Boggs said.

"Yeah."

"It was a general inoculation, bred from a space virus. It wasn't tetanus."

"So the doctors were liars," Dagger said.

"Yes," Boggs said. "Many people have lied and done bad things to get you and me here. But here we are."

Boggs felt a twinge of dizziness as he stood. Not good. He hadn't been eating enough, or drinking enough. And now he didn't care at all.

"Sir," Dagger said. "You don't look so good."

"I'm fine," Boggs said, lying through his teeth.

He went into the weapons locker, making sure the other Havoc 12 was in there.

It was.

He'd wanted to grab Portman's, but it had been covered in venom, and was already deteriorating at the edges of the casing.

Dagger stood, and took a drink from his nutrient straw.

"I'm sorry about Dr. Tara," Dagger said. "Real sorry."

"It's not anything to apologize for," Boggs said. "We did what we could. The security just wasn't good enough."

"The spitters are smart," Dagger said. "We couldn't have predicted that."

"We couldn't have predicated a lot of things," Boggs said.

Dagger looked sheepishly at Boggs. "So what's next?"

Boggs paused for a long time-or at least what felt like a long time. He reluctantly took a sip of his nutrient straw and struggled to keep the liquid down. His heart throbbed numbly in his chest, his jaw tight with stress.

"We wait for the spitters to clear the perimeter of Base Camp One, and we salvage what we can from CAV-121. Then we have to find a new place, and wait for reinforcements."

Boggs typed in a message on the console keyboard, marked it URGENT, and sent it to CPB headquarters.

"We're the last," Dagger said. "The last of the tip of the spear."

"Try not to think about it," Boggs said, with the weight of Mawholla in his voice. "It won't do you any good, Dagger. You're a sharp kid. I want you on your toes, quick and cat-like. I'm going to need you. Hell, the human race needs you. Got it?"

"Yes sir," Dagger said.

Boggs reached for his LifeForm meter, and his ZR-15.

"Get your equipment in order, soldier," he said to Dagger. "We have a mission at first light."

"Yes sir,"

Dagger said. "What is it, if I may ask?"

"We're going to finish the wire sample traps Dr. Tara had us set up on Pine Tree Ridge. She was on to something, and I want to find out what."

Boggs opened the bay ramp, and let the cool night air into the CAV. Then he walked out and smoked one of Dagger's cigarettes. As he did, he thought of Dr. Tara's beautiful green eyes, and how she was perhaps the most intelligent person he'd ever known. He just wished he'd gotten to know her so much better.

Boggs turned to Dagger. "Let's try and get some shut eye," he said. "We're not going out there in the dark."

30.

The two suns crested over Pine Tree Ridge, which loomed a good two miles in the distance. Pastel red and orange hues coated the sky and land. The serenity soothed Boggs as he tried to wipe away the memory of Dr. Tara. But he knew he never would. He could only numbly blot it out for a moment, like an eclipse. For as long as he lived.

Dagger hiked at his side, holding up his ZR-15, cigarette dangling from his mouth.

Boggs had to admire the kid's utter strength. It was remarkable. He didn't mope, he didn't get depressed. Sure, the kid would verbalize his negative emotions, but they were brief, not something dwelled upon…more like a curious, good natured animal than a bitter man.

God damn Boggs respected that.

Soon they reached Pine Tree Ridge, and began the hike uphill. They entered the clump of trees, and Boggs veered towards the barbed wire trap he'd set up with Dr. Tara. And sure enough, just like she'd said, tufts of fur were ensnared in the barbs. No blood, as the animal wasn't wounded at all. But plenty of fur.

Boggs plucked the fur tufts off the barbed wire with tweezers, and placed them into a plastic bag. Then he zipped the baggie into his pack, and headed uphill a few dozen yards.

"What are you looking for, sir?" Dagger said.

"Prints," Boggs said.

"Jekyll's?" Dagger asked.

"Could be anything," Boggs said. But deep inside he knew it was true. That's what he was looking for. He wanted to see the creature again, maybe figure out how it got so fast. Maybe it was something in the creature's diet. A long shot, but who knew on Mawholla.

After scouring the area for prints and taking photos, Boggs and Dagger hiked back to the CAV.

"Danni," Boggs said as he entered the ship, "take us to Base Camp One."

A wave of negative emotions roiled inside Boggs, as he balled his fingers into fists. He fought back tears. This was no time to be a bitch. This was go time. The CAV-121 was loaded with resources he and Dagger would need to survive the next few months. But not only survive, to also *learn*. Which of course would twist back into survival.

Still, Base Camp 1, and the dangerous forest surrounding it was the last place he wanted to be.

31.

The CAV landed directly in the center of Base Camp 1, close enough to the CAV-121 to make trips back and forth as easy as possible.

The laser fence remained in place. But it only stood as a stark reminder at how easily it had been manipulated by an intelligent species. The obvious answer was to make the fence have a roof, as well. A major design flaw by the CPB engineers.

Boggs and Dagger walked past Portman's remains. His head had melted away into his shoulders like a used candle. The Havoc 12 he'd carried was corroded and likely poisonous to the touch.

Boggs and Dagger opened the CAV-121 ramp with the remote device Boggs had taken earlier, and stepped inside.

Despite the exterior and engine damage, the inside was okay give or take a few flashing warning lights.

Then Boggs stepped towards the console deck, which looked like it had been spray painted by a wild artist whose favorite color was crimson.

He ignored the evidence of violence as best he could, and fished out the animal hair from the sample bags. Then he placed them inside what looked to be a microwave, but really was a sample analysis station.

Boggs waited, keeping his eyes as tight to the sample computer's readout as he could. He would not look at what had been done to his people in here. Could not.

At last the LCD readout on the sample device flashed, and indicated, as Boggs assumed, "unknown species". Then the computer displayed a bunch of stats and figures Boggs wasn't familiar with.

When it was over, the machine spit out a memory card with the data, and Boggs inserted the card into his portable LifeForm unit. Dr. Tara had told him this was a way to reinforce and enhance the data the LifeForm could retrieve in the field.

Next, Boggs and Dagger began the tedious process of resourcing what they could from the CAV-121, and what they could leave behind on the ship for future use.

The good thing about the CAVs was they used a combination of solar power and hydrogen to keep their onboard systems functioning. The CAV-121, if not messed with, would remain a long time in its current state.

After making a dozen trips between both ships, Boggs sealed up the CAV-121, and then went inside the 117 with Dagger.

"Sir, what are we going to do?" Dagger asked.

"We're going to do exactly what we do," Boggs said. "We are the spearhead. We will continue to explore and document dangerous species. We will execute the mission we are being paid to do. We will continue, Dagger. Come rain, or sorrow, or death. We are the Recon Elite. We DO NOT SHIRK, Dagger. We confront challenges, and we overcome."

"Yes sir!" Dagger said. "Are we going to go after the spitters?" he asked.

"Fucking a' right," Boggs said. "Time to stop playing prevent defense."

32.

The CAV-117 glimmered in the afternoon suns, just as it emerged from the thick band of clouds that covered the lower elevation valleys. Boggs piloted the ship past the high meadow where the crigs and spitters had battled, and set the ship to hover mode, perpendicular to the cliff.

Boggs had Dagger lower the ramp from the cabin, and he walked halfway down with a Havoc-12.

A big momma peered out from a giant cave entrance. Boggs pressed the trigger halfway, and the Havoc indicated a lock had been made. The bullet made a loud THUNK as it left the tube and accelerated towards the spitter cave.

Boggs loaded another bullet, and simply reinitiated the original lock, and fired.

"Fuck yeah," Dagger shouted from the cabin.

The second bullet rocketed into the same cave as the first. Boggs took the Havoc off his shoulder and waited for what was coming next. Spitters poured out from the rest of the caves, like a herd of disturbed deer. Two Havoc bullets followed them.

Boggs took control of the CAV from Danni, and positioned it a hundred feet over the fleeing spitters. Then he opened fire on the herd with the external canons.

Dagger balanced himself on the ramp, tossing down frag nades that imploded twenty feet over the spitters' heads. Some of the spitters reared back and hissed, trying to hit the CAV with venom, but the ship was too high for that tactic to work.

Boggs maneuvered the CAV fifty feet over the fleeing spitters, careful not to ram into the geological horn. He unloaded on them all with a cold precision. The combination of frag nades, canon fire, and Havoc bullets was too much for the spitters. Many of them lay dead and twisted on the tundra, some still alive as they squirmed and hissed. The first bullet Boggs had fired from the Havoc 12 fizzled out, and crashed. The second bore into the skull of a big momma, and exited out an eye in a viscous mess. Then it streaked towards the sky and exploded.

"Havoc bullets down," Dagger said.

Boggs maneuvered the CAV back to the cliff base, and the tunnel entrances. As the fleeing spitters tried to return, Dagger dropped frag nades on their heads from an altitude of approximately eighty feet. The nade concussions roared off the cliff wall, and shucked loose slabs of rock. One thing was for sure, Mawholla had never seen anything like it.

And it was in this moment that Boggs realized he had played it wrong. He'd let sentimentality get the best of him when he should've been more aggressive all along. They'd played an awful lot of prevent defense since coming to Mawholla.

Only a few spitters made it back to the caves.

Boggs flew the CAV close to the injured spitters, and had Dagger light them up with his ZR-15 from the ramp.

"Alright," Dagger said between bursts of gunfire. "This is more like it."

After a few more minutes, Dagger yelled that he'd gotten them all.

"Get back in here," Boggs ordered through the speakers.

Dagger ran back up the ramp, grinning all the while. He slammed the ramp button, and then slid the ZR-15 off his shoulder. "Man, about time we got those fuckers back," he said.

Boggs was glad to finally see the kid happy. He was inspirational, in a way.

"Let's get out of here," Boggs said as he piloted the CAV away from the high meadows and cliffs. Endless mountains stretched out before them as they flew just above the fog that obscured the valley and Base Camp 1. Boggs didn't want to think about that place. Not right now.

"Where to sir?" Dagger said.

"Anywhere we want," Boggs said.

As the CAV flew higher, Boggs viewed a series of maps on the touch screen console. Much of Mawholla was this rainforest ecosystem. Followed by the oceans, and the tundra on the north and south poles.

Dagger pointed at a map on the screen. "That looks like a super volcano or something," he said.

Boggs concurred. And it was an hour northwest of their current location, and on the way back to the tundra where they'd set the fur sample traps. For some reason, that area kept calling to Boggs. He couldn't shake the thought of Jekyll's shape on the horizon, shimmering beneath the two suns as the creature trotted towards Pine Tree Ridge.

But this time, they'd be heading to the super volcano. On the map, the caldera appeared to be at least forty miles wide. Similar to the Yellowstone caldera.

After an hour of flight, the CAV landed on the outer edge. But from the naked eye, Boggs couldn't really see the caldera. The area was mostly meadow and skinny-looking pine trees. Far off, mountains ringed the caldera, forming a scenic wonderland.

Boggs took a deep breath, and realized it made sense now. The trees on Pine Tree Ridge grew there at their furthest northern reach. That's why they were small and stunted. But here the same species of tree grew taller, and in thicker groves.

Boggs' mind flashed back to Jekyll, and how the creature always seemed to head for the trees. He wondered if this was Jekyll's species habitat. Or if Jekyll was an outlier. If so, how could that even be? The last of his species?

Boggs and Dagger emerged from the CAV. Danni had insisted his readings indicated the caldera was stable.

For now.

With their packs on, their ZR-15s, and a fresh brace of frag nades, they made their way west. The land was drier here than back at Base Camp 1, the pervasive heaviness of the humidity completely gone.

Boggs unfolded a small drone from his backpack, and flung it into the air. The drone whirred off to the west at eighty yards ahead of their position. When it reached the tree line, the LifeForm meter beeped. The drone had picked up something, the screen showing a figure designated as neutral.

"Could be anything," Dagger said. "You know, sometimes I really prefer being on the ship."

"The ship is our training wheels," Boggs said. "To truly know Mawholla, to truly provide value to this mission and CPB, we need to experience this planet with our eyes, with our noses, with our hearts."

"Yeah, that's nice and all," Dagger said. "But people seem to die a lot."

There was nothing Boggs could say to that.

The air here smelled of rotten eggs, and immediately Boggs knew it was the sulfur from all the geothermal activity. They had to be extremely careful where they stepped. Little wisps of steam rose up from the earth in random spots. At times, it felt like walking on a baked pie.

"Look at this shit," Dagger said, pointing at a small pool of boiling water. "Crazy."

Boggs stopped hiking. Dagger followed.

"We should've run a scan," Boggs said.

He took out his LifeForm meter and ran a geological scan. The results were better than he thought. Although the area was very active, the ground should still be stable enough to support bipedal figures (IE humans). Basically, the hike would be one long visual assessment test. As long as they had their wits about them, the risk was generally low.

The LifeForm meter beeped, and auto-switched to biological mode. The drone was sending back an image….an image Boggs did not care for, at all.

The creature looked like a grizzly bear at first, but loomed larger at the shoulders and overall height. The thing had a face that seemed to be a hybrid of a tiger and a hyena, with big, cat-like eyes and sharper ears. It was hard to tell from the drone captures, but it looked to be eight feet tall.

While on all fours.

Dagger snuck a peek at the LifeForm screen. "Jesus," he said. "You have got to be kidding me. Biggest bear I've ever seen."

Boggs nodded. "It makes sense," he said. "The fauna here is very similar to Earth, and the life zones. And I'm guessing that's the case for a lot of non-desert planets that are still capable of hosting vibrant life."

The LifeForm meter beeped back at the men, indicating the bear as "dangerous".

"No shit," Dagger said.

The men angled past a bathtub-sized hot spring, the water at the top light blue, then clear, then a dark concentration of blue near the sinkhole.

"How far off is the bear?" Dagger said.

"Sixty yards to the northwest," Boggs said. "We're going northeast along the tree line here to avoid it."

"Good," Dagger said.

As the men made their way along the tree line, Boggs realized the meadow was a meadow for a reason. The trees didn't grow in it, because the roots would be scalded. Boggs cut just inside the tree line, by about fifteen feet, and worked northeast that way.

The LifeForm beeped again, and scrolled text across the screen: WARNING – PICTURED SPECIES MAY BE AN EDGE SPECIES, RELYING ON AMBUSH BASED UPON INITIAL PHYSICAL EXAMINTATION.

"Oh, that's fantastic," Dagger said.

Boggs checked his six, and looked around.

The LifeForm meter beeped again: WARNING. DANGEROUS SPECIES OFF RADAR.

Boggs looked around at the woods. He listened, but only heard the slow bubbling of a nearby spring. The forest was thick and spindly here, rows of trees imprinted upon rows.

He heard a branch snap, and turned to the west. Before he could react, the bear came charging through the woods, faster than any horse he'd ever seen.

Boggs spun and fired his ZR-15, but the gun was knocked out of his hands by an enormous paw. The thing's claws sliced his palm open, and blood oozed free.

Boggs heard a terrible WHUMP as the bear knocked the wind out of Dagger's lungs. Dagger hit the ground hard, the full weight of the bear on top of him. Boggs recovered his ZR-15 and fired repeatedly into the bear's haunches, but this only served to enrage the creature.

Boggs watched in horror as every time the bear was hit with a bullet, it tore at Dagger's face with its powerful jaws. The poor kid screamed over and over. Boggs pressed the trigger on the ZR-15 again, to no avail. He'd emptied the chamber.

The bear, now bloodied and limping, pried itself off Dagger and tried to run. The beast made it thirty feet out onto the meadow and collapsed, wisps of geothermal steam rising up behind it.

Boggs turned to Dagger. Most of his face had been ripped clean, leaving a terrifying mess of bone and exposed eyeballs. Dagger cried, blowing blood bubbles as he breathed.

His chest had been ripped open, revealing cracked ribs and a pulsing lung.

"We did good," Dagger said. "My p's would be proud, sir. Real proud."

Boggs looked down at his man, and finally let himself cry.

"You're going to be fine," Boggs said. "You just hang in there, kid. I want you to know-you were the best I ever had."

But Dagger could no longer talk.

Boggs picked up the kid's ZR-15, and aimed at his heart. Boggs had never, in his life, had to face such a thing. More than anything he just wanted to throw up.

But he couldn't shoot.

He couldn't shoot the kid while looking him in his eyes, or at that half-skeleton face. Instead Boggs de-pinned a frag nade, and placed it into Dagger's palm.

"I'll see you soon," Boggs said. Then he turned and ran through the woods to the west, never looking back as a violent explosion ripped through the caldera.

33.

Boggs wrapped his injured hand in gauze from the CAV med supply, after dabbing an anti-bacterial ointment into the wound.

His hand hurt like hell, but not as badly as his heart. Everyone was gone. His best chance at love after Sarah had died. His trusty Recon Elite. The only thing he had now was time, and the hope that the planned reinforcements would arrive as scheduled.

Boggs limped out of the CAV and into the meadow. A hundred yards out, the dead hump of the bear rose like an anthill. Boggs carried with him a shovel, and dragged behind him the bagged bodies of Dr. Tara and Dr. Volter.

After a lot of digging under the two hot suns, he was able to lower the bodies of all three into the ground. Then he covered them and smoothed out the dirt. He jabbed a broken branch at the head of each grave, and carved their names into the wood, as well as their lifespan details which he'd procured from the onboard computers on the CAV.

Boggs stood from his work, his bandages coated in dirt and blood. He didn't feel the cut, or anything really. Just a crushing numbness. He took great, heaving breaths of Mawholla air, and shook his fist at the two suns.

Then he headed back to the CAV, and slept for two days.

34.

He woke, starving and thirsty. He sucked at a nutrient straw, then put on some coffee. The gentle purring of the life systems on the CAV could be heard in the background while he stretched his sore muscles.

Slowly, surely, dark thoughts crept into his mind. The sudden loss of companionship was overwhelming. He was alone. Well, maybe not entirely.

"Danni, what day is it?" Boggs asked.

"It's Thursday," Danni said. "Within the context of Mawholla's spin, which is precisely 37 hours, 13 minutes, and 8 seconds."

"Thank you," Boggs said. "It's good to hear your voice again, Danni."

"Thank you, Captain. I'm glad you have risen from your sleep. It was a long one."

Boggs nodded and stretched his lat muscles. He'd kinked them up during sleep. Then the cramping began, deep in his calves. He went to scream, and tried his best to stop the cramps by flexing his muscles. This only made things worse.

Dehydration, Boggs thought. *Things like magnesium and potassium were important, dumbass.*

Boggs sucked on his nutrient straw and waited a minute, stiff on his bed. Soon, his muscle cramps relaxed and he was able to stand properly, and without pain.

As he brushed off the mental cobwebs, Boggs thought of his missing people. The void was palpable, to the point he wanted to vomit back up his nutrient drink.

He had to shake it off, had to move on, had to survive. His survival depended on his mental acuity. What he needed to do, no, what he *must do* was focus on his work.

Boggs reached for a camera he'd taken from the biologist's ship, and his COMM device. With no biologists, and no Recon Elite, Boggs made the decision that he'd be both while he waited for reinforcements.

He organized a backpack full of gear and nutrients, a tent, sleeping bag, LifeForm meter, a Havoc 12, a ZR-15, a drone, and numerous frag nades. He was a walking god damn pile of equipment. And that was fine.

"Danni, I need you to run a tight ship around here for a while," Boggs said. "I'm going to be gone for a week, maybe more. Run things as you see fit, but please stay put unless you notice geothermal irregularities."

"Understood, Captain," Danni said from the speakers. "Is there anything else you'd like me to do?"

"Yes," Boggs said. "Start the beacon so CAV-125 and CAV-129 can find me."

"Initiated," Danni said.

Boggs opened the ramp, then met the day.

He walked forty yards into the meadow, and hit the remote trigger, and the CAV ramp slowly closed.

Boggs headed towards the dead bear, then began taking photos of it, from head, side, other side, and paws. Then he spoke into his COMM device in record mode: "Calling this species, Tiliar," he said. "Eight feet high at the shoulders, when on all fours. A head the size of a Kodiak bear, with the face of a tiger, minus the stripes. Claws appear to be eight inches in length, made of keratin, like on Earth. The bear sustained at least thirty rounds from the ZR-15 rifles before succumbing to the wounds. Hard to say if we were at fault for invading the bear's territory. Sex is female. Certainly, it's a dangerous animal. But not as dangerous as the spitters. This is a species that can co-exist, if proper educational tools are implemented. We may have surprised her."

Boggs set the COMM device aside, and took a deep breath. Dagger's blood was all over the bear's muzzle, making it hard to continue.

Boggs got to his feet and headed northeast. He wasn't sure exactly why. A feeling, a ghost-thought compelled him to do so. He was simply going to explore, document, and learn about Mawholla, to be of use to those coming next. It was his mission, his purpose, and now, the only thing that mattered in his life...the only thing that was real.

He hiked for hours through a ravine of pine, rising above the caldera. The LifeForm meter beeped off all sorts of creatures, from squirrels, to snakes, to smaller versions of Tiliar.

He crossed rushing creeks swarming with fat, colorful fish. He entered slot canyons, found himself trapped, and turned around. Small wildcats followed him, then dispersed into the brush when he turned to look. Crow-like birds fluttered overhead on occasion, cawing out to other forest creatures.

He moved his way north, mile after mile. The two suns set, and he found himself camping on a high plateau, overlooking a massive canyon tipped with the pine trees. He set up his tent at the base of a large rock, then gathered downed wood and sparked a campfire. He drank from his nutrient straw and stared up at the heavens. He did not wonder at the stars the way he did on Earth. He'd crossed them. They were no longer a mystery, just another highway.

Mawholla, however, was something else entirely.

He woke in the night many times. Creatures scurried near his tent, or on it. Bat-like wings fluttered in the dark and picked off insects. The THUMP THUMP of a chunky rodent-like animal.

In and out of sleep he drifted, dreaming of Sarah, of Dr. Tara, of Dagger and Portman and his deceased crew. He didn't remember their deaths, only their healthy, smiling faces.

It occurred to Boggs that he'd had a good run. He wasn't old, really, in terms of years. But he sure had a hell of a lot of miles on him.

In the middle of the night, his LifeForm meter beeped. Before sleeping, Boggs had sent the drone up, so it could guard a perimeter around his campsite. Boggs rose at once, shedding the sleeping bag off his skin. The meter showed a vague shape skulking between trees, a hundred feet from his current position. Based on the contrast with the trees, he assumed the species to be cat-like in nature, perhaps the size of what had been known as "leopards" on Earth.

Boggs reached for his ZR-15, then climbed atop a boulder that stood ten feet off the ground.

He had to make a decision, and soon. CPB had trained him to, at the very least, observe an animal's behavior. The next step was to ascertain a danger level beyond what the LifeForm interpreted. He was taught that in many instances, predators could be scared away by loud noises. However in some instances, making noise could attract a predator.

Boggs waited in the dark, his LifeForm meter blinking in front of him as the creature skulked closer.

Boggs gripped his ZR-15, fully prepared to put a bullet between the eyes of whatever it was. He saw its eyes glimmering back there in the campfire light. He aimed his ZR-15, but before he could fire an awful shriek filled the night. It echoed across the plateau and down into the badlands, sounding like the call of some tormented banshee, or maybe a woman's scream through a distortion filter.

When Boggs looked back where the creature had been, the eyes were gone.

Cute, he thought. The creature was capable of throwing its voice.

Boggs checked the LifeForm meter, but there was no indication the species was anywhere to be found.

It had simply disappeared.

Perhaps it was one of those predators that would rather run and hide then stay and fight.

Boggs heard the drone whirring lightly overhead as it made yet another pass. Then he crouched back into his tent, and slid into the sleeping bag.

He woke every ten minutes, sitting upright, listening as much as he could as his heart pounded in his throat. The wild of Mawholla pummeled him over and over again. It occurred to Boggs that when he'd wondered about Jekyll being the last of his species, that he was merely projecting his own fears. Now, he was the last.

He shook it off. Tried to shake it off. Must shake it off. There was work to do. And he was going to do it.

At last Boggs closed his eyes, safe in the comfort of the LifeForm device and the circling drone. He ran his fingers along the tent wall, marveling at the fact this was his first night on Mawholla without a metal wall between himself and the world. It made him feel closer.

35.

The morning was colder than he'd thought it would be, his breath leaving his lips in moist, visible clouds.

Boggs poured some instant coffee into a tin cup, and sat it amongst the fire embers.

While it heated, he broke down camp and packed everything into his backpack, which hung on him like a wounded person. Far below him, to the north the mountains faded, revealing a vast forest like the one where Dagger had been killed. Except the trees grew shorter, and not as thick. It reminded him of another place on Mawholla, one that kept drawing him back.

Boggs scrambled down the plateau, kicking loose rocks. He crossed a river, and dodged many geothermal pools. Sometimes he heard the sound of bubbling as steam mist rose up in ribbons through the forest.

He spent all day traveling north. He poured sweat as the two suns cooked him, and he had to pack away his down jacket to lighter layers.

He came across numerous animals...all of them neutral. Variations of squirrels and salmon-looking fish that swam upstream into tiny rivulets, where they splashed their tails against the gravel, creating spawning reds.

All around him the wild beauty of Mawholla stretched. Pure, untamed. Never-before-seen by man. Ever.

He set up camp in a patch of stunted trees, next to a creek the fish were spawning in. He caught two of them with his hand while laying prone on the bank, and roasted them on a stick over a fire.

As he ate the flesh, Boggs stared into the flames. Strange things were happening to him. He was finding himself getting lost in it all. He did not feel the need to fight, to battle, to destroy. He was simply a part of Mawholla now. He would die here. He knew that.

Always knew that.

His belly had not been full like this in a long, long time. He dozed off, not bothering to unfold the drone and have it patrol the perimeter.

In the morning he broke camp, and heard rustling along the creek. Two of the Tiliar creatures fished for the spawners, slapping the water with great paws.

Boggs reached for the Havoc, but the bears didn't care about him. They had their food, they were occupied with more pressing matters.

Boggs wondered if the big bear that had taken Dagger's life was simply territorial. Or if something had been wrong with it. Maybe its fishing skills had diminished, and it was desperate.

Boggs snapped photos of the bears, and planned to document a few details orally with the COMM later.

When he finished, he threw on his backpack and headed north.

In the evening, after countless creeks and bogs, the geothermal features started to fade, revealing a near-desert badlands full of red and green rocks. The colors were beautiful, reflecting dusk as the two suns set.

The mountains had long gone now, replaced by these small plateaus interspersed with dry grasslands.

Boggs made his way through a ravine and sipped his nutrient straw. He thought he heard something behind him, and stopped.

The thing tried to slow its movement in time to match Boggs, but it was clumsy.

Boggs turned around with his ZR-15 ready to go.

A large four legged animal stared at him.

A lerka.

It eyed him, keeping its long snout snapped shut.

Fuck, Boggs thought.

As the lerka stared, several more lerkas appeared from the stunted trees.

Boggs counted at least a dozen.

He backed away slowly, lowered the ZR-15, and dropped his pack. The lerkas watched him hungrily, then leapt from their positions.

Boggs had the Havoc 12 out of the pack in two seconds, already pressing the trigger. The Havoc had previously established a profile on the lerkas, so the lock initiated faster. The bullet made a loud THUNK as it rocketed out the tube, and into the face of the first lerka, knocking its head clean off. Then the bullet slowed and angled back.

Boggs really wished he'd found the portable laser shields they'd had. But now was not the time to wonder. He dropped the Havoc and aimed the ZR-15 at the next charging lerka, right between the lerka's eyes. But the next lerka was too fast, and he felt its bizarre jaw tear into his right shoulder, smelled the wild urine stink of it.

The Havoc 12 bullet doubled back and killed the lerka behind the one attacking Boggs. Boggs tried to twist his arm away, only worsening his injuries.

He was able to cut at the lerka's eyes with his camp knife, forcing the lerka to back off. Boggs heard awful growling and roaring as the Havoc 12 bullet continued its work, maiming lerkas outside his peripheral vision.

Another lerka seized his right leg, and Boggs stabbed at its eyes, popping one of them as if a crushed grape. The lerka roared and retreated.

Boggs got to his knees and released a frag nade towards what remained of the lerkas. As he did, one came in behind him, and seized him by the neck.

I'm dead, Boggs thought. *I'm fucking dead.*

The lerka tossed him around, letting go of his neck and flinging him onto the dusty crust of Mawholla.

They came for him then, all three remaining lerkas. The Havoc bullet streaked skyward, and disappeared.

"See you soon, Sarah," Boggs said to no one.

But the lerkas stopped.

They were staring at something behind him.

A banshee-like cry wailed throughout the badlands, and Boggs turned to look. There, not ten feet behind him stood a creature with a wolf-like snout and curious eyes. It cocked its head, as if wondering what to do.

Or maybe not.

"Jekyll," Boggs muttered.

Jekyll disappeared, and not a second later one of the lerkas whimpered.

And then another.

For the briefest of moments Jekyll would appear, and then disappear, only to be followed by an ear-piercing whimper, as if the lerkas were a dog that had been brutally scolded by its owner.

The lerkas couldn't take any more of it, and fled the mini-canyon, not bothering to glance back.

Boggs looked up, and Jekyll was standing above him. The creature cocked its head at him, and let out quiet purring sounds.

He tried to stand, and Jekyll backed away.

Boggs held a hand to his throat, and pulled back his bloody fingers. The cut didn't feel too deep. His leg hurt like hell though, like the skin had been torn off. And sure enough, the bite had ripped apart the ankle area of his pants, and he was bleeding pretty good.

As Boggs took out the portable med kit and patched himself up with gauze and anti-bacterial ointment, Jekyll watched him from fifty feet away.

"What do you want from me?" Boggs asked.

Jekyll went to all fours and then back into a bipedal position, while crying out strange, almost language-like vocalizations.

Yet, Jekyll waited for Boggs...waited for him to gather his things and follow.

Boggs stood, and did just that. But first he had to stash the Havoc 12 under a clump of trees. There were no bullets left. He attached a tiny location tracker to the underside of the Havoc, and activated it. A tiny beep emitted. Whenever he got back to the CAV (if he did), he'd be able to find its precise location using special homing equipment.

Pain shot up Boggs' leg, and now he was starting to feel it in his neck. He took a couple aspirin and washed them down with his nutrient drink.

He limped along, towards Jekyll, who moved further and further ahead of him, yet never quite leaving his line of sight.

Boggs pulled out his LifeForm meter, but it had been damaged in the lerka fight. Which meant the drone was gone too, flying around directionless without the homing signals of the LifeForm.

Boggs set the LifeForm under the boughs of a tree. He could retrieve it later, and try a repair. But for now, the meter was just unnecessary weight.

He began to shed other things he didn't need, too, and set them beside the meter.

Feeling wounded but lighter, Boggs could now sort-of keep pace with Jekyll, who was leading him north.

36.

They walked into the night, until Boggs couldn't stand it anymore. He made camp in a group of stunted pine-like trees, similar to the tundra area where he'd first seen Jekyll.

He gathered twigs and sticks and even a few dried logs from the ground, and made a campfire.

Jekyll stood atop a rock shelf that formed a sandy "V" behind camp. The creature just stared at him and cocked its head, making the unusual vocalization noises.

Boggs realized Jekyll was now his personal drone, his new LifeForm meter.

He took more ibuprofen, and tended to his wounds. Then he took a flask he'd gotten from Dagger's bag, and drank heavily. The wooziness pleased him. It was good to be soft around the edges sometimes.

The pain in his legs receded, and his neck didn't feel half bad.

He fell asleep thinking of Sarah. She was leaning over him and kissing him on the cheek. *Hang in there*, she said to him.*Hang in there.*

37.

The next morning Jekyll was waiting for Boggs patiently at the edge of camp. The creature glanced up at the two suns, then let out strange vocalizations.

Boggs packed everything away, and walked towards Jekyll. Jekyll scooted away at a pace faster than Boggs was capable of. He winced at the pain in his leg and neck. This was a sore, throbbing pain opposed to the bright pain on the day he received the injuries. He wondered if he was getting an infection.

He wondered a lot of things.

But ever since that day in the worm tunnel, Boggs had a funny feeling about Jekyll. And he had to admit, he didn't feel as alone.

An hour later Jekyll disappeared out of sight. When Boggs made his way through the trees, he glimpsed a muddy, narrow creek, and heard splashing. Jekyll emerged from the creek, his fur matted down to the skin, looking rather peculiar. Jekyll held a fish in his mouth that resembled a catfish.

Jekyll whipped the writhing fish at Boggs, and Boggs had to dodge the damn thing.

The fish thudded to Mawholla, and gasped for air. Boggs quickly put his camp knife through its head, and held it out in front of him, the slick, glistening fish making two last flips before dying.

Jekyll stared at Boggs, head cocked, and made a weird barking sound.

"Have to cook it," Boggs said. "Humans cannot eat raw. Well, maybe they can. I just won't unless I'm starving."

Jekyll opened and closed his wolf-like snout, and cocked his head sideways at Boggs.

"Maybe later," Boggs said. "Thank you, though."

As Boggs got ready to continue the hike, Jekyll disappeared, and then appeared directly to Bogg's left. Jekyll swiped the fish off the knife, disappeared, and reappeared fifty feet ahead of him with the fish gripped tightly in his front paws.

Boggs shook his head.

It never, ever got old.

38.

When the two suns dipped behind the horizon, Boggs set up camp. In the morning the badlands diminished, instead replaced by low, grassy hills and sparser trees. The smell of the country was familiar to Boggs. It was the start of the tundra.

He drank from his nutrient straw and had a few snack bars he'd been saving in his backpack. The soreness from his wounds faded, and he felt his strength rising again.

Jekyll began pulling away from him, growing smaller and closer to the distant horizon. The thinning trees made it much easier to see long distance. Boggs used his binoculars to keep track of Jekyll, and occasionally shouted out to him. But the animal would only look back briefly, and then continue on his way.

39.

In the evening, in the dusk of two suns, Boggs found himself walking down Pine Tree Ridge. Far ahead on the horizon trotted Jekyll.

Boggs called out to him. "Hey, where you going?"

Jekyll stopped and looked back at Boggs, head cocked, wolf-like jaw making near-language inflections. The creature moved faster and faster to the horizon, and then was gone.

Boggs sat down and cradled his hands with his head. He let out a sigh, and checked to see if Jekyll had come back.

But he did not.

Pristine wind sang through the stunted pine trees, and sighed in the tundra grass.

Mawholla called to him. Sara and Connor called to him. Dagger, Staunch, Portman, and Dr. Tara called to him.

Boggs took a deep breath, and answered.

"I'm here," he said. "I'm right here."

END

CHECK OUT OTHER GREAT SCIENCE FICTION BOOKS

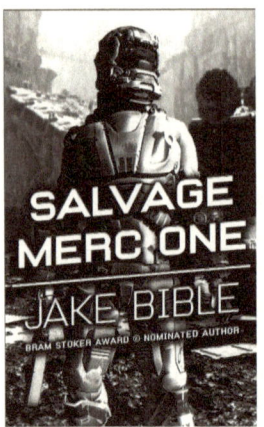

SALVAGE MERC ONE
by Jake Bible

Joseph Laribeau was born to be a Marine in the Galactic Fleet. He was born to fight the alien enemies known as the Skrang Alliance and travel the galaxy doing his duty as a Marine Sergeant. But when the War ended and Joe found himself medically discharged, the best job ever was over and he never thought he'd find his way again.

Then a beautiful alien walked into his life and offered him a chance at something even greater than the Fleet, a chance to serve with the Salvage Merc Corp.

Now known as Salvage Merc One Eighty-Four, Joe Laribeau is given the ultimate assignment by the SMC bosses. To his surprise it is neither a military nor a corporate salvage. Rather, Joe has to risk his life for one of his own. He has to find and bring back the legend that started the Corp.

SERENGETI
by J.B. Rockwell

It was supposed to be an easy job: find the Dark Star Revolution Starships, destroy them, and go home. But a booby-trapped vessel decimates the Meridian Alliance fleet, leaving Serengeti—a Valkyrie class warship with a sentient AI brain—on her own; wrecked and abandoned in an empty expanse of space. On the edge of total failure, Serengeti thinks only of her crew. She herds the survivors into a lifeboat, intending to sling them into space. But the escape pod sticks in her belly, locking the cryogenically frozen crew inside.

Then a scavenger ship arrives to pick Serengeti's bones clean. Her engines dead, her guns long silenced, Serengeti and her last two robots must find a way to fight the scavengers off and save the crew trapped inside her.

CHECK OUT OTHER GREAT
SCIENCE FICTION BOOKS

MAUSOLEUM 2069
by Rick Jones

Political dignitaries including the President of the Federation gather for a ceremony onboard Mausoleum 2069. But when a cloud of interstellar dust passes through the galaxy and eclipses Earth, the tenants within the walls of Mausoleum 2069 are reborn and the undead begin to rise. As the struggle between life and death onboard the mausoleum develops, Eriq Wyman, a one-time member of a Special ops team called the Force Elite, is given the task to lead the President to the safety of Earth. But is Earth like Mausoleum 2069? A landscape of the living dead? Has the war of the Apocalypse finally begun? With so many questions there is only one certainty: in space there is nowhere to run and nowhere to hide.

RED CARBON
by D.J. Goodman

Diamonds have been discovered on Mars.

After years of neglect to space programs around the world, a ruthless corporation has made it to the Red Planet first, establishing their own mining operation with its own rules and laws, its own class system, and little oversight from Earth. Conditions are harsh, but its people have learned how to make the Martian colony home.

But something has gone catastrophically wrong on Earth. As the colony leaders try to cover it up, hacker Leah Hartnup is getting suspicious. Her boundless curiosity will lead her to a horrifying truth: they are cut off, possibly forever. There are no more supplies coming. There will be no more support. There is no more mission to accomplish. All that's left is one goal: survival.

CHECK OUT OTHER GREAT SCIENCE FICTION BOOKS

IN PERPETUITY
by Jake Bible

For two thousand years, Earth and her many colonies across the galaxy have fought against the Estelian menace. Having faced overwhelming losses, the CSC has instituted the largest military draft ever, conscripting millions into the battle against the aliens. Major Bartram North has been tasked with the unenviable task of coordinating the military education of hundreds of thousands of recruits and turning them into troops ready to fight and die for the cause.

As Major North struggles to maintain a training pace that the CSC insists upon, he realizes something isn't right on the Perpetuity. But before he can investigate, the station dissolves into madness brought on by the physical booster known as pharma. Unfortunately for Major North, that is not the only nightmare he faces- an armada of Estelian warships is on the edge of the solar system and headed right for Earth!

BATTLEFIELD MARS
by David Robbins

Several centuries into the future, Earth has established three colonies on Mars. No indigenous life has been discovered, and humankind looks forward to making the Red Planet their own.

Then 'something' emerges out of a long-extinct volcano and doesn't like what the humans are doing.

Captain Archard Rahn, United Nations Interplanetary Corps, tries to stem the rising tide of slaughter. But the Martians are more than they seem, and it isn't long before Mars erupts in all-out war.

www.ingramcontent.com/pod-product-compliance
Lightning Source LLC
Chambersburg PA
CBHW051950170626
46808CB00007B/2551